UNTHOLOGY 9

UNTHANK

First Published in 2017

by Unthank Books

All Rights Reserved. A CIP record for this
book is available from the British Library. Any
resemblance to persons fictional or real who are
living or dead is purely coincidental.

ISBN 978-1-910061-44-2

Edited by Ashley Stokes and Robin Jones

Book and Jacket Design by Robot Mascot
www.robotmascot.co.uk

www.unthankbooks.com

CONTENTS

INTRODUCTION

Welcome to the Archipelago.

Stare out to sea for too long and they will leave without you. They will trudge back through the dunes to the cafés and the beach huts, the tat and the fossil shops. They will have already started to pity you and will do so for as long as they still remember you. Realising this will be humbling and humiliating, but you will continue to stare at the horizon – the shimmer of it, the haze – until the the now-speedy little waves lap at your toes. Soon they will cover your ankles.

Before the beach becomes a sandbar and the sandbar the seabed, you will know that you could go back. There is no forwards, only backwards, so you will go forwards. You will stagger, wade, stomp, wary of rocks and crabs and the spines of weaver fish until your feet are lifted from the rippled sand and there will no longer be any need to beware what lies beneath.

Out you will go.

Dunked, bobbing, surrendered to the flow, you will realise that if you carried on in the way you had carried on, this was always going to happen.

The beach will soon be far behind. The forgetting will have begun. You will feel a certain panic when you appreciate that it's now not so much a case of how much further forwards you can coast, but of when you will be sucked under.

There will be islands in the distance that you know you could never reach. There will be wrecks and reefs and rigs and sea forts but in the glare, in your state of mind and surrender how can you know that they are not illusions and will keep receding the closer you get. Manta rays will glide beneath your feet. Your splash will disturb squid and cuttlefish. Shark fins will take angular circuits around you. Something monstrous and cold will appear to be following in your wake, but you will not have the nerve to look back. You will wonder if there really are cities beneath the waves, Thonis-Heracleion, Phanagoria, R'lyeh, the domains of Old Leech and his Stepford Cuckoos, his Hermetic Order of the Purple Swastika. They want you. Want you to go down.

You will want to sink now, to be freed somewhere down there in the cracks and the sediment that swirls and drifts, descends and flattens.

What you have that passes for strength will finally wane. As you plunge, all the traps will release you: the trap of birth, the trap of love, the trap of sex, the trap of work, the trap of debt, the trap of childhood, the trap of adulthood, the trap of family, the trap of appetite, the trap of hate, the trap of the body, the trap of history, the trap of opinion, the trap of ambition, the trap of identity, the trap of will, the trap of time, the trap of the self, the trap of life. All their springs and mechanisms will dissolve in the murk that is rushing to engulf you.

Some time later you will surface, gasping, emptied, and there, from some dingy or platform someone, some smudged visage, a blur in the mist will hold out an understanding hand.

Welcome to the Unthology Archipelago. Anything to declare?

I

ROSIE GAILOR

*"The thought that I might kill myself formed in my mind
coolly as a tree or a flower."*

Sylvia Plath

Apparently drowning is the most euphoric way to die.
The brain starves of oxygen and thinks back to every
memory you've ever had – even ones you'd thought you'd
forgotten – to see if there's anything to save you. It recalls
everything, completely out of your control. I think of it as
getting to watch a movie of your life for free. I slip out of
my dressing gown; the bath is ready. A bottle of *gamma
hydroxybutyric* is placed inconspicuously amongst my
shower gel and shampoo (the man I bought it from said
its street name was 'Soap' and I can't deny the sense of
satisfaction it gives me). The water embraces my body, wet
and warm. How much of this 'Soap' am I meant to use? It's
dripping from the flannel now, thick droplets falling from
the cloth into the bathwater. I think I'm using too much…
Though it's not like it'll matter, in the end. The now-damp

flannel is cool against my skin. It smells like hospitals; its clinical aroma claws its way up my nostrils. I close my eyes and imagine the Soap wringing my nerves, turning my muscles limp. I can hear the steady hammering of the builders working next door; *tang, tang, tang.* I can still wiggle my toes. How long does it take to work? *Tang, tang, tang.* The relaxing motion of my head bobbing in the water makes me feel sleepy. My arm starts to feel numb. I can't move my fingers. My toes spasm before they start to tingle, and I watch them as I submerge under the water. *Tang, tang, tang.* I feel warm. My dark hair wraps itself around my neck and face as my body slowly floats and sinks; floats and sinks; floats and sinks in the water. If I could smile, I would be smiling. If only I'd thought to put some music on. I can feel my limbs jolt and jerk as the water burns in my lungs but I ignore it and watch the birds outside the window. The door is unlocked so I can be found; windows ajar, food thrown out, rubbish in the outside bins. I don't want to be any trouble. But *damn* – I didn't hang out the washing to dry. It's too late to go and do it now. The water begins to sting my eyes and I can't close my eyelids, now the water's turning grey and ashen, thickening around my body and morphing into concrete-

I'm walking down some stairs – I'm in a rush – why didn't I take the elevator? Somewhere to go… but where? No time to remember. I'm practically running, taking two steps at a time and, *shit,* yes, that's right, the elevator was broken so I had to take the stairs. I'm just out of the building door when a flyer is shoved in my face, a burst of red and green pillaging my eyes. *What the fuck?* I remember yelling, anger and frustration and *there's somewhere I've got to be.* A do-gooder, yes, that's it, hence the table with the boxes and bags and what looked like a pair of heels belonging to a transvestite – bundles of clothes for donation. A name badge – what did it say? *Marvin.* Well, Marvin, thanks but *no* thanks. Beggars can't be choosers and they certainly can't choose to ask me for what I damn well earned. *Charity?* Where the fuck is charity this morning when I'm running late for this sodding meeting in – where the hell is this place? Yelling, anger, frustration spinning around my head with a blur of noise accosting my ears –

(Thank god I'm under water; I dread to think of the racket
I'm causing)

– My clothes are *my* clothes, numbskull. If they want some they can bloody wait until some woman who's just lost seven stone chucks out her old wardrobe and *buys* new clothes with her *money* so she can throw *her titbits* to your dogs. I don't want to help them out or do you a favour or give that away. It's *mine.* You got that? *Mine.*

Thrashing, air bubbles, spasm upon spasm and my eyes are
wide open-

WHERE IS THAT NOISE COMING FROM? Bright lights are flashing, my chest vibrating, my best friend holding my wrists and jumping up and down – 24. 24 years old. *Can you believe this?* I can't believe it. I haven't seen her in *years.* We're at a bar – by the bar – orders given, drinks received (too many to carry; we had to drink some as we stood). *Get some more. My body can't breathe so let's drown it some more.* Vodka, rum, tequila, schnapps. One o'clock, two o'clock, three o'clock, four. Minutes passing but I can still smell that fucking Soap – get me something, babe, I'm thirsty. *(It's not as if I'm surrounded by water, right?)* She gets me a shot of something – tastes like bleach – burns my throat but *sweet mercy* it's more fun than thinking where my body really is. We take a pill – I can't remember if it's blue or purple but I just swallow it like aspirin and don't give a fuck - dancing like I'm in a Madonna video, thrusting and grinding and not caring that my skirt's around my hips it's my fucking *birthday.* Paying for a round on my credit card for us and the cute guys dressed up as Ancient Greeks – nearly a month's wages – money never better well spent. Drink after drink after drink until I feel so full I may burst or it'll start spilling out of my ears. Someone spills their drink – all over my hair – ice and all – like a wave of

water lapping at my feet when I was eight years old. Mallorca, I think. A fuzzy-framed memory, rose-tinted, sea-side holidays and family fun, going back to a time when I didn't care about anything apart from wasting time. There was some Spanish boy with his family beside us – but we had deck chairs and he didn't. I sat in my chair like a throne. I should have had a crown. *Go and ask him to play.* An annoying buzz, a fly, maybe? *Go and ask that little boy to play with you.* Just the wind and the crashing waves. *Did you hear me?* My eight year old self stares my mother in the face, her jolly smile illuminating her tanned features. I do as she says, I always do; there's no arguing with my mother. He doesn't speak English – *surprise, surprise* – but I start making a mound from the sand and he understands. The universal language of 'child'. He uses his hands, like an ape, an Aborigine, an un-evolved caveman. I go back to my family and pick up my bucket and spade – he takes no notice, now fully immersed in my mound. I start another one; sculpt it into a castle, now with a moat, now with turrets, now with water in the moat, now with shells as windows, and *mummy, look!* A sandy wall protecting my creation. No one will harm it under pain of death; I will look after the keep until the sun sets and we get cold. The Spanish boy looks at my masterpiece. He wants to copy it. He can't copy my castle. He's just a stupid caveman. He comes over and gestures towards my spade. *No, you stupid ape, you can't have my tools. I am a sculptor and you are a brute. You don't deserve it.* When no-one is looking I kick sand at his face and he doesn't return after that but I don't care, because every person who walks past admires my castle and I am sitting beside it beaming with a smug smile because it's *my* castle and it's mine until the sun sets and we have to go home.

I look out of the window. The birds are gone.
The hot water scalds my eyes as I'm pulled down –
I'm in my office, my prison, my cage. That smarmy girl with the see-through blouse and the rouged cheeks is parading

to the front of the crowd. How *dare* she? She shakes hands with our boss and I can practically feel his erection pressing against his trousers. He doesn't even *try* to disguise his eyes looking through her shirt. That sodding tart with my sodding promotion. (*I don't remember being this angry.*) She acts like she doesn't expect it and *oh my god, I got it? No way!* Fake and conceited and smug, so smug, rubbing it in my face. Blood boiling and brimming in my skull, pushing red through my skin. Hotter and hotter, my skin feels like it'll ignite any second. Everyone sits down at their desks and I fight my way through the crowd congratulating her – a friendly congratulatory coffee? *Oh I'd love some.* Coffee it is; with a little extra that I'll give you for free. In the company kitchen – with the door shut firmly behind me – the kettle boils – I'll make the coffee extra strong in case she tastes it. Damn, where's the first aid drawer? I had always laughed when I saw the laxative sachets in there whenever I went to get a plaster but *dear lord* it's a blessing right now. One sachet – enough? No, two, always go for more if unsure. Two sachets in her mug of coffee: extra strong, extra sweet - extra sweet revenge that is. I almost bring it to my lips to make sure the taste is undetectable, *whoops*. I stop myself just in time. She won't know what's hit her. I hope she doesn't even make it to the toilet. Public humiliation for the newly-promoted air-head. Coffee handed over *–thanks, doll* – and I wait. The people disperse; she's waiting for it to cool; I can barely contain my irate glee; first sip. She's drinking it steadily now; sip, sip, sip, sip, *come on*, she finishes the mug. *Sweet mercy.* I cannot stop letting out a cackle behind my notebook – I become the smug one now. Her eyes are bulging as she clasps her stomach and runs out of the office, down the corridor - I can imagine her locking the toilet door now – I hope she took some air freshener in with her. I tell the boss I'm leaving early, walk past the toilets, *congratulations again on the promotion.* I could practically hear her breakfast and my extra-sweet coffee spill out of her, eyes bulging and cheeks flushed-

Air bubbles gush out of me like an insult you can't take back. I can only watch as they grow and burst in a mad torrent. It's beautiful, really. A tragic ending with the gushing and the rushing and the swirling and the dizziness and the thickness of the water as I try to breathe it in, like breathing in honey, sweet and sticky, and-

It even smells like you. Manly and musky and rugged and tough. Stubble, dark, thick; eyes, blue, piercing; hair, lustrous and hazel; tanned and tall and *overpower me*. Behind the door, lock it, turn around, fuck, *yes,* you pop off one of my buttons, don't care – look for it later on the waterlogged carpet but never find it – kisses hot and hard, *there. Make sure no one's watching.* I was always ashamed. The cheap fucks in dark corners, never the romantic dinner in soft candlelight. The bathwater fills my mouth and as he kisses me it runs down our chins. I hated him; and I hated myself so much I'd let him to whatever the fuck he liked to me just as a reminder of how low I'd sunk. My knickers don't even leave my legs, hanging around my ankle so that whenever I looked at them I'd think of the man who took them off. My hand slips on the ceramic walls, the room flickers between being a bathtub and the office supply cupboard. Thick moans escape from his throat. *I* did that. *Me.* It's powerful. I feel powerful and weak at the same time. Open and closed, private and on display. Water is running down the walls as my liquid coffin starts to encase me. Hot skin against hot skin, brush my hair back and *god you smell so good* – hands here and there and *yes – there* – sweat and your boxers are around your feet and your dick is swollen and I'm ready *god I'm so ready* – low tones and I forget where I am and breathe in; water cascades into my lungs and I sink further. You're whispering in my ear *my name, say my name* – bubbles float up from his mouth as he speaks - thick and full and pushed against the wall and my hands run through your hair. Eyes are locked and I can't look away; vision is blurred so I imagine you fucking me on my desk, always have, never will; too obvious. Better to be behind closed doors like a secret you're proud to be ashamed of. *Say it again. Say it again.* Powerful hands slipping over my body and strong words making bubbles and a manly man claiming my body and I don't care because in my mind we've done this a thousand times. Every time you walk past me it's a new position; a new place; a new scenario. Droplets of water pour from the ceiling and I can't tell if it's romantic or scary or both at the same time. Bubbles blind me – your hair feels damp with sweat and it's rolling down your back and your neck – *the feeling is starting to come back in my fingers but I won't scratch my way out* – I bury my head in your neck; I don't want to see it – I don't want to be there when it happens. *I can't believe I didn't put the washing out* – I draw your arms around me and for the first time since I stepped into my watery escape route I start to feel...scared. You smell of the Soap. My heart is trying to beat its way out of my rib cage and the prickling in my fingertips spreads to my toes and my lungs feel like they're about to *burst* and I wish the Soap would numb my nerves as well as my muscles but I'm burning alive and freezing to death at the same time. I can only lie and watch the violent flow of bubbles that are leaving me behind. *Say my name, say my name.* But you don't know it. You can't say it. I can't tear myself away from your eyes, in disbelief; I start to choke and you laugh. You *laugh.* I sink my fingertips into your back and I'm panting and gasping and water is tumbling out of my mouth but you're still *fucking me*. You're groaning into my ear and I'm trying to close my eyes and forget about what I'm hiding from but the water is creeping down the wall, intent on catching up with me. My hair fans out in the pool of water climbing up our skin, your wet hands are rubbing against my skin, and you push me down farther. We sink. You're the weight on my chest that I'd never noticed before. Your hands lock around my throat and I'm closing up, and I'm scared, but I won't close my eyes. The lights are flickering above us and the photocopier that I've always wanted to fuck you on is sparking. Droplets of water spill onto the surface of the water, making ripples, *Soap, Soap, Soap.* Your skin is drenched, and you're kissing me, and I want to tell you to *stop* – to please just *hold me* - but all that comes out of my mouth is a gush of tepid water, and the tears that I want to cry don't have time to fall before the water around us turns to ink, thick and black and all-encompassing. It tickles and burns at the same time. I'm drifting from everything I've ever known, and I'm glad, because this is the first time I've felt anything other than lost.

MAY DAY

SJ BUTLER

Harry falls into shivering sunlight, twigs snap sharp under his feet, and the wind roars like wild surf up in the treetops, lifting him back to the ocean

He saw it just the once – the enormous breathing shining mass of it, so huge even his father stopped – though his father stopped for nothing – and held his hand. 'That's the sea, boy'

From that day it swelled inside him and each night he rocked on the waves and counted the days till he could sail away and when it was time he used Ma's best pen, black ink, and his hand shook before making the first mark

His hands are warm from the sun through the window. He lifts one, holds it close, sees loose skin, stained with all his years like the papers in the tin, the layers of his life – marriage, births, and death – and in amongst them the form, its final section still blank where his father refused to sign

Father.

You'll be a baker, boy. That's our business.

So he hauled the delivery bike daily up Bird in Hand Street and over the three fields to Ashurst, loaves warm in the creaking baskets front and back, the smell of home ahead of him all the way. In summer the waving corn closed behind him, leaving no wake; ahead, it seethed, whirlpools where hedge-end and hill-side twisted the breeze. He pushed through it, legs itching from the sharp-edged grainheads, cycling over the brow and down the valley towards May at the Anchor. Every day he did it, till at last May came with him to the beech copse, lime-fresh leaves swaying high above them, making an undersea world below: they ran, swimming in strands of sapling-seaweed that stretched up above them to the surface. And she didn't pull away or laugh at him, she weaved through the stems, her hair streaming in the current and then she stopped, pulled him to her and whispered,

Don't be afraid of falling

She's the only one he ever told.

And all those years of rising before dawn to bake cake after cake after cake – his father's cake man, famous in all the villages, and in the end even in the town, for the feather-light fluff of his sponge – he still dreamed

Of high winds

Of sailing towards, never to – you never know where your boat and the wind will take you

Of leaning into the wave on a curl and dipping his fingers into the glistening freezing water, leaving a small trail of popping bubbles behind him, of licking the salt and knowing he's

Home, where May brought him tea in bed every morning, and whispered 'sail happy' into his ear as he left for work

where her friends settled in the kitchen like gulls, chattering, pecking apart the life of the village around them over cup after cup of tea

You make a good cake, Harry, they'd say, and sometimes he'd whip up eggs and butter, sugar and vanilla from Madagascar into a storm just for May, and as she ate it he'd dream of deep blue harbours and the welcome of strangers who'd swim out to him bringing baskets of mangoes and bananas, and he'd say to her, it's not the best I've made

The best? The birthday galleon whose sides were a hundred sawn logs of chocolate shortbread, its three oak masts gleaming caramel, and its rigging a singing complexity of spun sugar. May sewed a flag for the mizzenmast, and together they carried it in, and gave their boy the weight and freedom of their dreams, and May turned to touch his hand

May with a sprig of May blossom in her hair, white against her neat black curls

May leaving the room, shoulders hunched and slamming the kitchen door behind her

His Father in the kitchen doorway. Grow up and face reality, dreams don't pay the bills, boy.

Did Father ever dream? Deep in the shed, shoulder to the world, perhaps he did and told no one, on days when the wind blew wet from the west and the sea was in his hair

Harry hears the surf and in amongst it, the sounds of May Day: everyone is up and out, hanging bunting, baking cakes: sponges, loaves and biscuits are rising all around him in a street of ovens and open kitchen doors. The children are screaming, high on cake mix and the excitement of the fair. Next door's is burning – her oven is fifteen degrees too hot, he can tell – in a minute she'll be running out into the garden with a smoking sponge, wailing why does it always burn on the outside and sink in the middle? She might have asked May, but how would she know he's the one? He used to teach the girls in the street how to bake a perfect Victoria and ice it, one hand under the cake, the other stroking the buttercream into smooth perfection – they'd all come round, and May'd make them tea

They don't come now May's gone. May's friends brought casseroles and crumbles for a while, and a salad and pie on Saturdays to last him through the weekend but in the end they left him alone

so he sits by the garden window with his tea, his eyes in the tree tops, dreaming and swimming till a child's voice cries, My ball! My ball! and a red blur flies softly in the wind, veering this way and that as the gusts take it. It lands in the top of his birch tree and he knows no one will dare come round for it, not in this wind. Not that he minds – when the wind's high and the clouds higher, it's always been easy to dream, to feel the sails above him white against the blue, the pull and suck of the sea, the jolt of the quayside

Ma's hand, wrapped warm round his. 'Never mind Harry, look it's sailing off to find treasure and adventure. Let's watch it till we can't see it any more.' And his new red ball carried high by the surf, in and out, like a dancer in the hall, toeing, dipping, turning in the sun, and at last caught by a curl of green glass water taller than him, and lifted out and beyond the surf to the whale waves, 'I saw a picture of a whale once, Harry, its back was as long as our house, imagine – it looked just like that wave.' And he didn't cry, he wanted to follow his ball, out into the green grey mystery, and he and Ma stayed there till it dipped one last time behind a ridge of water and out of sight. 'What an adventure,' Ma said. 'Not many boys can say their ball has sailed for America, can they?'

He'll fetch it, maybe, if the wind drops

though the chimney's sighing: today the gulls will flee the gales inland, angry tourists screeching above the village green, scaring the cats off the fences

they used to be peg-toothed affairs you could poke an arm through, or a leg, and Father could step over. May painted their fence blue

pulled him into her dream – of a house to ourselves and children to tuck up at night, and a pot of tea on the kitchen table to share with friends, a sherry on Sundays. But his own dream always hung just above them, sometimes a barely-there wisp of summer cloud, other times a boiling mass of black, blocking out the children's drawings on the wall and her smile from the stove where she always was, stirring, mixing, making. She thought he'd put it away. Hung it up alongside his tools, drawn round it to mark its spot. Tidied it when she called him in for tea. But that's not where it was

He can dream all day now

in the branches the ball hovers, an evening sun that's forgotten to set, red against the blue in its net. The branches are holding it up, stopping time. What did May used to say? Time and tide wait for no man. He pulls himself out of his chair and walks through to the kitchen, no need to see, his hands graze the rough and tweedy back of his chair, the cold edge of the wall where it turns for the passage, the low shelf and the miniature plates, painted china animals, pictures, pictures, pictures of the children. The wind's getting up. It's moaning in the slates and fireplace, breathing the smell of damp soot through the rooms, that reminder that summer's not yet here

He pours. Milk, tea and his dram of whisky that turns it to rust and fire

Father sold the business, left Harry a cake man without an oven, said he wasn't the man for the job, head in the clouds, so here's Harry in the delivery man's cottage, the only thing left to him, with its chips of blue white china poking through the grass, sown the summer May and his sister tried to run a tea garden, not that they minded when no one came

May Day, they'd set up in the institute the pair of them, with a ring of friends, a pot of tea, a plate of scones – never as good as their own, mind, but you have to go and play your part

the ball's still there, though the sky's beginning to darken so it's more like a bruise now, it's up in the rigging, a beacon sending its signal

he learned them all, the signals: black and yellow flag for quarantine, blue square with white within – the blue peter – we're about to leave, come on board – hung his own from his bedroom window in case a sailor happened past, heading for the coast and in need of company

and two red lights, one above the other, for run aground,

the sun and the ball, sending out their signal

blood in the water

oceans in the sky, every drop of rain that has ever fallen on him has once been ocean

he'll climb the mast, swing up into the tallest cross bar and out into the blue with the wind, just two toes touching the rigging, his hands outstretched in the endlessness of out there

he follows the threads of his house with his fingertips along the corridor and through the kitchen, the counter, the swag of bags by the door, their crackle, the rattle of keys, and out into the wind

its insistence, its won't take no for an answer demand that he run despite it all, the dazzle through the yellow of his eyes, platches of tree, light, sky, a slash of green, he'd forgotten the sheer noise of outside, the many-ness of it, the birds, children, bamboo racketing in the blow, wind in his ears, bare feet, twists of grass between his toes, nettles his mother's cool hands on his hot legs, soothing the rash, letting him go, hands outstretched like anemones alert for any feel of fish or net or tree

and through it all he finds the tree, grips its rough bark – that same bark he'd cut into with his new knife on his ninth birthday, placed his hand on the bark and sliced round it, as high as he could reach, sawing till he could clearly see his fingers outlined, the sap bleeding clear under his palm

year by year his hand left him behind, climbed away from him, reached up for the clear blue, the heavy grey and the howling wind without him

where is it? He reaches but there's no hand. He leans in, snuffs the must, the earthy greenness of the old tree, wraps his arms as far round the trunk as he can stretch. It binds him, roots him, strands him as it always has. All those cakes and tea-times and doors closed against the wind and rain, his back turned against the whale waves carrying his ball away again and again this time he'll follow, he'll sail within the silence of the wind's own breath to where there are no limits and he'll find his ball

he pulls away from the mooring of the tree and lets his memory guide him, creaks the shed door open and there's a scuttling, he smells dried soil and rust, can see nothing, but knows where it is and seizes the ladder, wrestling it free, Ha!

He leans it against the trunk, nudging its shoulders into the widest bark cracks, wise enough still, in this moment, to take care

don't be afraid of falling

the bark cuts into his skin as he grips its coral edges, frilled where it stretched and broke as the tree grew, turned by the years into something almost stone, but living, he can feel it, he forces his fingers into its cracks and beetle holes, breathes in the khaki smell of mould, and curls his toes round a rung, clings his arms about the massive trunk

has it grown, expanded into the night? Is it breathing too with the waves below?

he toes the rung above, pushes up, face pressed against bark, eyes shut, heart punching his chest and throat, throws one arm up

feels a branch with his finger tips

swings his weight and just as he's about to fall

catches hold, pulls himself up, feet scrabbling for tiny holds, hears the ladder clatter to the ground and someone else must surely hear, come running, tell him to stop, but the night silence steadies itself again and he knows no one will know where he is or where he's going

he's away and falling doesn't matter

he lifts an arm and finds another branch above, holds it tight, legs and arms shaking

he breathes, letting the current rock him, the breeze float round him, cool him, slow the heaving of his chest until he is ready

it's so dark he can see neither sea nor sky

but his body remembers, his arms and legs reach and leap as he climbs up and up till he stands tall, breathing slow and sure, eyes open in the night, catching the glitter of silver fish under the moon

he places his left hand against the trunk, smoother here, less torn and stretched apart by the years, and he feels the outline of a hand

its palm and fingers are clear, its curves, lines, ridges and bumps are his

palm to palm, they breathe the salt breeze, hear the green swell below

hand in hand, they climb higher and higher, they swing with the waves, on and on, till there's nowhere to fall, and nothing to hold but air, and he lets go

BREATHLESS

JANE ROBERTS

Sometimes she finds it so hard to breathe. Oxygen. It's like love. It's all around. Somewhere. Invisible. Like God. Or Christ. Or the Holy Ghost. Or whoever, whatever. It isn't as if she believes in all that. So on some days it's hard to believe that there's oxygen. And when she broods on this thought, the air around her thins…catches…like bits of scratchy wool… in her throat…around her tonsils…drying…clogging… suffocating. Everything parched. Throat closes in. She keeps… swallowing…but the tacky flesh…keeps…adhering together. Until –

'Becca? Becca, can you hear me? You're having another panic attack.'

That's him. Tom. That's love. That's oxygen.

Her throat relaxes, becomes unstuck. Her heart rate decelerates as he places and secures the oxygen mask gently over her mouth and nose once more. The rush of aerated reality, the touch of his solicitous fingertips calms her. Helpless in almost every way, her eyeballs roll up to the monitor alive with pulsing green electrical snakes to the side of her bed.

Science. It's all around her. She eases her weary head, neck and shoulders back into the starched cotton hospital pillow. The S-shape of her backbone uncurls – painfully – on the rigid mattress; she's not as agile as those green snakes on the monitor. Machines and computers – controls where she has no control anymore – constantly drone on above her head, below her feet, to her right, to her left – all four points of a virtual crucifix covered. In these breathless, panicked moments – the ones before she realises he's still there – all she can do is turn to contemplation.

*

Is there a science to love? she wonders. Certainly, science makes their love possible now. A formula. Formulas are needed for most things. She thinks back to when he left her. Thinks about the things she did to herself. The things she neglected to do to herself, for herself. Had that been a formula to win him back? Or had she just been waiting till self-destruct mode mutated into outright annihilation? Whatever, it worked. Secretly, she was pleased with the conclusion of all that damaging thought and action. He was back. They were together. Everything was OK again. All this goodness from a mere phone call after months of leaving messages that had seemingly been lost to a greedy answer machine, forever eating up her love.

'Tom, it's me. Please, don't hang up. I've got something to tell you.'

She remembers how factual she became on the phone, how this feeling of power grew with each sharp intake of breath on the other end of the line, each muffled sob.

Tom moved in that week. She opened the front door and he scooped her up into his arms like a cliché Prince Charming in a fairy tale or a Mills and Boon. She didn't mind the pain of his clenched grip around her fragile limbs; she could only feel and breathe in the lightness, the sudden freshening of everything.

'It's all going to be fine, just fine,' he said.

And then he ventilated the rooms to get rid of the stench of rotten tobacco. One of the reasons he left; now one of the reasons he's returned. He made a special calendar of all the appointments. He set out the copious boxes of pills in order, labelled them with tags she could understand better. He made sure she had everything she could possibly need for the hospital.

Cancer. Love. Oxygen. They're all around. Some in shorter supply than others. You have to know how to access these supplies; you have to realise when they have run their course.

*

In the night she awakens and he's not there. It's her worst fear. Like when she used to wake up when he first left her all those months ago. She looks around for him, feeling her skin goosebump and prickle in the chill. And yet it's the hottest July the country has had for twenty years – even in the small hours, heat and sweat filters out into the atmosphere from all surfaces – whether animal, vegetable, mineral, or man-made construction. She doesn't know what she is, where she is: the plastic water jug that she can barely hold herself now isn't by her side in her eye-line; gone are the beeps and pings of the chattering machines and monitors; she's losing all sensation of that chill.

And then a scene appears before her, laid out as straight and flat as the sheets on her bed. There he is. Tom. He's still there. Waiting by her bed. But his body is drooped, overcome. The tightness of the atmosphere is tinged with silent lament. And the terror becomes real in a way she had never imagined in all of her best-laid plans. It is not he who now is absent.

MOTES

MARK MAYES

i

I was rejected from every job I applied for, so I became a dust collector. I'll tell you about it. I saw the advert online and sent in my curriculum vitae as an attachment and a few words in the body of the email about how hard-working I was, which is an odd thing to say because I hadn't had a job for nearly three years. I suppose I was saying that I was potentially hardworking. The reality is, or was, that I am not sure at all whether I ever wanted to work hard. I wanted to work soft. But where would anyone find a job that asks for that? Or even if there was a soft-working job going they would never advertise it as that. You have to be in the know, to be in the network, have the right contacts to get into a soft-working job, which is always advertised to outsiders as hard working. Hard workers won't get it, of course, even though they say they want hard workers. A soft worker will get it. A soft worker with the right tone and bone structure and history.

So I applied to be a dust collector. How hard could it be? I got a call about ten one night. Quite late, I thought. I'd given up hope of hearing, actually. A bloke with a sort of posh voice, but with an undertone of roughness, said I was to come to Perbury the following Tuesday, at two in the afternoon, and meet him in the lounge bar of the Green Fish, and we'd go through the necessaries, as he put it.

There was a bus from Folburn to Perbury at twelve thirty-six. I'd have about an hour to kill and then hopefully the bloke would turn up. He said he was paying by the hour but he didn't say how much, even when I lightly pressed him. 'It's variable,' he said. 'Depends where you do it. And when you do it.' He seemed in a hurry to get off the line. I knew my place. I was the beggar here, so I left it at that.

When I'd told the Borg, which was my name for the Jobcentre eejits, that I had an interview to be a dust collector, they said, 'Oh, a refuse collector, well, that's good, that's good, especially in this economic climate.'

'Not refuse,' I said. 'Dust.'

'Yes, dustman. Dustperson,' the lady with red-framed glasses intoned, a bit pompously, I thought. She had a purple gonk on her desk. I thought about picking it up and running out the door. Something made her move it behind her mug, which was printed with a picture of a castle in Wales. She pointed to the relevant section on the black screen with white text, which told me I would be paid up to the appropriate date. 'Smashing,' I told her. 'Thanks for all your help. I'll keep trying.'

I got up, and she goes: 'Good luck with the interview. You might be collecting my bin. I'll look out for you, Mr Tripp.'

'I haven't got it yet. Anyway, it's not bins. It's dust.'

She shrugged. 'Good luck then. And remember your u.s.p.'s.'

I must have looked like I didn't know what she meant. But sadly I did.

'Unique Selling Points,' she said, then flashed me an offensive grin. 'Make *them* want *you*.'

I made some kind of noise, and left.

Anyhow, enough about all that. You don't need to know everything about me. I mean, I haven't told you how tall I am, my racial background, my eye colour, whether I have a withered arm or not. But you can still see me sort of, can't you? I am a man looking for a job. Or at least, I was. Maybe you've been in the same position, so you can relate, no? Ugh – I won't do that again, the 'no' thing. Hate it when people do that at the end of a question. Funny how we adopt little things what we say we hate.

ii

I'd never been in The Green Fish. It was an old place, small, snugs, heavy looking chairs and tables, wonky black-painted beams, a fire in the grate, even though it was April. Near the fire, a raggedy terrier lay by a metal bowl filled with small biscuits. The creature looked dead. Then I caught it breathing.

I sat on this round corner table under the dull horse brasses. I had a pint of Eagle's Nest. Not a bad ale, and one I'd never tried. They were using Sauvin hops, apparently, giving a tropical fruit finish leading to a long bitter note in the mouth. The back of the beer mat told me so.

The guy at the bar had been foreign. I suppose he still was. When I mentioned the nice weather to him, he shrugged, then brushed his arm like he was brushing away a cobweb. He had a mole just under one eye. Music came faintly from some speaker somewhere. This, too, was foreign. It sounded a bit Eastern, and I quite liked the beat, if they call it the beat in those places. Now and again a dumpy woman from what I presumed was the kitchen of the pub came out to the bar and whispered something in the barman's ear. She was a lot shorter than him and had to stretch up, her hand cupped round her mouth, to reach his lug. They were youngish, involved, I suppose. Having sex. I tried to picture it. No one else was there.

Harry, he didn't give his last name, the man hiring dust collectors, or perhaps just one dust collector, would be due any minute, providing he was punctual. I expected someone a bit fat, getting on, reddish face, tweedy sort of bloke, the kind of shoes that you have re-soled rather than chuck. That's what his voice had said to me. I also expected him to have hair sprouting out of his nose. I can't say why – images just appear, don't they? We're not responsible for them. Like dreams.

Then the door creaked open. I noticed a change on the face of the barman, an opening of his whole face, not surprise, more the impersonation of surprise. A character shuffled in. It was a woman. Tallish, long grey coat, long grey hair, shoes that were more like slippers, untidy. Not quite a bag lady. A blue canvas bag was slung over her shoulder. Late fifties, I thought. Her, not the bag. She glanced round the place, as if expecting someone to be waiting for her. She took me in briefly, but gave no sign of acknowledgement or greeting. Her face was tanned, lined. One of her eyes glinted in the low light. The dog sprang up silently and went to her, wagging its stumpy tail. The woman stepped forward, stooping, fussed its ears, under its neck. Then the dog returned to its imitation of a corpse near the fire, and lay there as if it had never moved.

'Coffee, strong, touch of milk, no sugar?' said the barman.

'You're getting to know me too well,' she replied.

The barman brought two long bony fingers to his forehead, then gave a small salute and disappeared through the half-open door on the other side of the bar.

I became aware of the woman looking at me. It wasn't a challenge exactly, but it wasn't indisputably friendly either. 'Afternoon,' I said.

She seemed to sum me up for a moment, as if she was making an important choice whether to speak or keep her silence. 'Harry can't make it. Something came up. You'll need to make do with me.' She broke her stare, then walked over to a larger oblong table nearer the bar, and sat down. Then she said, without looking at me, 'Do you mind relocating, so to speak? That table's a bit pokey. I like space.'

'Oh, right, the job. Yeah, I'm here to meet Harry about it.' I stood, picked up my briefcase and pint, and made my way over.

'I think we've established that. Take a pew.' She extended a pale, ringless hand, indicating one of the chairs.

I held my hand out to her, but she gave a quick shake of the head. 'No need for that,' said the sort of posh voice. Sort of posh like Harry's had been. A voice used to telling creatures where to sit, and when. A doggy lover's voice.

I wanted to leave at that point. Maybe I should have done. I'd come across rude interviewers before, where they were just going through the motions, some even yawning during their set questions, some so over friendly, but frighteningly vacant behind the eyes, so that you knew it was a no go within two minutes. Or they might give you the sense that you'd failed before you'd begun. I went to one where the guy made it clear he thought it was weird that I was applying for a job as a waitress for his charming little bistro, even though he shouldn't have been specifying the gender of the employee sought. I reminded him of that, and it was downhill from there.

I had to keep going, cap in hand, to these no hopers to keep the Borg happy, to show I was willing to consider anything, always, and within twenty-four hours notice, forever. The vital thing was to keep the money coming in, without which I would potentially starve, or actually starve, although no one actually starved in this country, they said. But where else would the money for food come from? How would I afford to even wipe my arse? But then if I wasn't eating I might not need to wipe my arse. No, realistically, I would be forced to steal, then I'd be put in prison, which might improve my educational opportunities, and perhaps I would come out into a better class of bedsit and become an outreach something or other. Or more likely I'd be victimised and end up hanging myself from a door jamb with a noose made from long tears of prison blankets twisted together.

I squeezed out a smile. Let's get this over with, I thought. I'd get my bus fare paid by the Borg, so I hadn't really lost anything. I sat down slowly, and consciously began to slow all my movements, as I'd read in a magazine that this gave you a higher status, or gave others the impression that you had a higher status than you had. When I'd first tried it, I think I overdid it, and someone interviewing me for a job as a traffic warden said, 'Is there something wrong with you, mate? You're moving in slow motion.' I was surprised he'd been so blunt as that, what with equal opps, but there you go. I had tried to snap out of it and began moving faster than normal to redress the balance. He wound up the interview quicksmart after that, and told me, with a bit of a sour look on his mug, that they would let me know. He didn't say who 'they' were. They never did let me know, whoever they were.

Back to the matter in hand. She locked eyes with mine. 'So, do you think you can do it?'

I felt my jaw tighten. I didn't say anything. I looked at my pint and thought about giving the old bat a good soaking.

'Are you up to it? Are you ready for it?' she said, her voice lower, her eyes pulling mine back into hers again.

I swallowed. 'Dust collector? Erm…well, to be honest, I don't know exactly what it is. What it entails, pardon my ignorance. Harry wasn't very precise about it. In fact, he told me very little indeed. But…'

'The clue is in the title.' She smiled now, and her teeth were good, perhaps a little too good.

I gave a small laugh, and her smile got wider, and she nodded slowly and a bit like a motorised thing, like I was getting something deep yet murky, which only she could tell me. Not getting it logically, but through some peculiar understanding.

'There you go, madame.'

It was the barman with the coffee. I hadn't been aware of his approach. He smelled of something floral. I looked up into his face. There was a foreign sadness there.

'Anudda?' he jerked his head toward my near empty glass.

I dug deep in my pocket. Ferreted. 'I'm not sure...'

'Get him another, and a single whisky, malt,' said the woman.

'It's alright,' I told her. 'I can buy my own drinks.'

The barman had already moved off. I fished out two fifty-pence pieces and a variety of fluff. I was keeping the fifties for the laundry driers.

'Don't be so proud, young man. Believe it or not, I, too, have been poor in my life. Have even been forced to beg, on occasion. Many years ago, I hasten to add.'

Is that what I am? I thought. 'Poor'. I'd never considered using that word about myself, but certainly it was true. I didn't own property. Or a car. Or shares. I was reliant on selling my time and, at best, my semi-skills, and my unskills for a survival rate of pay. But I wasn't even doing that. I was one of the *useless eaters* that I had read about once. The segment of the population that a government would ideally want to do away with, if their being there wasn't slightly more necessary than their not.

'Thanks,' I said. 'That's very kind of you.'

She blew a little air out the side of her mouth, as if my thanks were a tedious irrelevance. Then she rummaged into her bag and pulled out a black folder. She laid it on the table and opened it. 'Ah,' she said. Then she took the small almond-shaped biscuit from the saucer of the coffee cup and bit off a chunk. Crunch crunch, she went. She leafed through pages of print. I tried to read it upside down. It didn't look like proper writing. Maybe it was in another language. She ran her finger from right to left, and I remembered, from God knows where, that Arabic is read or written like that.

Then she looked up. 'Mr Tripp, let's get down to the nuts and bolts of the thing.'

I was beginning to feel fidgety. Something held me there. Not her. My interest, I suppose. This was new. 'Yes, let's do that,' I said.

Again the barman interrupted us. He banged my pint and a small glass of whisky down on the table. Then he did a thing I didn't quite like. He gave me a little slap on the upper arm. It was meant to appear to be a friendly slap, I suppose. But it hinted at an underlying aggression. And the aggression was that he had covered it by making it seem a type of friendly gesture. But the strength of the slap, the cold strength of it, made me take it the way it was rightly meant. I could have got up then. I could have pushed my thumbs into his eyes. Instead, I smiled. 'Thank you,' I said. He ambled off to his position behind the bar.

'You are familiar with dust?' said the woman. She held a gold fountain pen now, poised over a blank sheet of paper.

'I am,' I told her. 'I don't dust as much as I should. I let it build up. I'm with that gay fella who said it only gets to a certain thickness, and then it stops. What's his name?'

She ignored my question. 'Dust isn't usually collected, is it? So, can you tell me, briefly if you would, why you think we should consider you for the role of dust collector?'

'Well, I don't know why you want it collected,' I said, feeling a bit more in control of the situation. 'I mean, you advertised for one, and I turned up. I need some work, some money, a purpose. I could go on existing on the dole, but they're always on my back. They want me to get a job. Anything, they don't care. Even if I got a job torturing mice, or eating human shit eight hours a day, that would suit them. They don't care what I did as long as I did something.'

'I understand you, I really do. And so did Harry. That's why we invited you here. I won't waste any more time with these questions, was just doing it for form's sake. We got a whiff of potential off your résumé. A heady whiff. We think you could be right for this job. We know you are a contender. But we have to be absolutely sure. Not everyone is up to it. Not everyone would commit.'

'But what is it?' I said, raising my voice. 'Sorry, what is it?' I sipped at the whisky. *Laphroaig*. I could rarely afford it. Lovely taste. Like a distant belligerent sea. A smokey memory of lost darkening islands. A query for the perplexed, answered in the mouth, and the soft burny swallow. So that you sat back, and for a moment, or an hour, let go of the pain of being responsible for anything. Even your own thoughts. Especially those.

The woman placed her hand over one of mine. Surprisingly, I felt teary then, but held it back. She reminded me of who I wished my mother would have been. 'All it is, dear, is sitting there collecting dust. It's difficult but not complicated. It's like being a porcelain dog on a mantelpiece. Like a row of books that are never read. Like an unopened bottle of wine, given as an unwanted present. Like flowers in a funeral parlour. You let the dust…'

I tried to say something. She brought a finger to her lips. 'You let the dust settle on you. Allow it to drift from the upper air down over your body, and not try to avoid it, like most people do by their constant moving, their ugly frantic business. This dust, which is a mixture of human skins, yours and that of others, alive and dead, and innumerable other substances, which have broken down over centuries, or days: carpets, plant-life, notes to the milkman, iron ore, the emissions and residues of power stations and charnel houses, panda faeces, the pointless dreams of ants, wings of invisible bugs, clothes catalogues for fat people, parchment, gravestones, tax bills and fonts. I could go on, but it would be wasteful of time. Fundamentally, you let a fine, fine coating of enriched eternal dust fleck and pattern your hair, your beautiful fingers, your lapels, the curve of your ears, the tops of your brogues. You let it fall on you, like an inevitable grey rain. A patina. Nice word. A patina of time and turning will build on you, noticeable only to the wisest among us. Then when you've had enough, you get up, shake yourself like a wet dog, grab a shower, or simply let it fall away, or remain as it will, as you go about your day.'

I sat back, as if rocked by a well-deserved blow, pulling my hand away. 'You're mad,' I said. 'You're taking the piss out of me, because I'm a useless cunt. A sad soft cock. I'm a purposeless man. A useless eater. You're working for the Borg. You're one of them.'

Her mouth pursed, as if to say something. Then she gave a quick jerk of her chin. She spoke in a vicious whisper. 'We were right. We knew you'd be suited. We could hear the quiet desperation behind every line of your application. The desperation of the truth crying in a wildnerness of fools. You always were a dust collector. It's your métier, your calling. You were born for this. You have it. The thing so lacking in all those who have applied and failed, who didn't get past first post. You have *honour*.'

I got up to go.

She put up her hand like a stop sign. 'No, please, Mr Tripp, Andrew, give me one more minute.' She reached into the pocket of her coat and brought out a wad of notes. She peeled off eight twenties, counting them under her breath. 'One hundred and sixty pounds, Mr Tripp. Forty pounds a day over four days. For only two hours work on each of those days. Twenty pounds an hour. Not bad, you'll agree. Not too many hours to begin with. You can't go at this like a bull in a bakery. That will take you up to Friday, including today. Two hours of sitting there, in your kitchen or your bedroom, thinking whatever you like, just not doing anything, not moving too much. You must sit relatively still but you can stretch or let your head fall side to side. We're not monsters. You can look out the window, listen to the radio, or a recorded book, if that's your bag. As long as the dust settles on you, as long as you fulfil the role of a collector. Just try it, Mr Tripp. Give it four days. What have you to lose? Then come and meet me, or Harry, if he's available, here next week, same time and place, and we'll see how you've got on.' She spread her hands in an appeal that made her look like a saint from the Middle Ages, or some statue on a tomb.

I barely nodded.

She pushed the money across to my part of the table. I sat

back down.

'Are you serious?' I said.

'Give it a whirl. Trust in this. In us. We are serious people.'

'I don't know who you are,' I said. 'I don't know your name even. I don't care about you. I could take this money, and not do the dust collecting, and not come back again. Or else I could just say I'd done it. You'd be none the wiser. I could come back next week and get another payment. I could do that.'

'Ah, but you wouldn't do that, would you?'

I drank some of my second pint and began to feel a bit light headed. I'd not had any breakfast. I looked into her grey eyes. She might have been attractive once. She still was. She was beautiful on her own terms. She was mother, and the wife I would never know. I wiped my mouth and now I covered her hand with mine. Hers felt like there was an engine pushing her blood around. She vibrated. She shimmered with will. I got caught in the briar of her gaze, and I told her the truth. 'I wouldn't do that. I wouldn't do that, for I have got the honour.'

iii

And so, when I got back to my little pied-à-terre, as I laughably call it, I took off my coat, had a quick tea, then sat in the kitchenette, on the red stool. The afternoon sun did its best to last, and I watched it through the long, barred window. The beams of light lit up the particles falling. The particles of dust. Why they were falling, I don't know. Some were moving upwards, though, on currents of air or heat or something that I could not detect myself, but these particles were sensitive to it. I sat quite still, which is not a usual thing for me. Mostly, I twitch or blow my nose loudly, or fidget about. But watching the falling particles, the rising ones, the ones that kept around a similar plane, all doing their thing, well, it calmed me. It was a sort of meditation, I reckon, watching those…those *motes*, as I think the word goes. Motes.

And of course, these were only the visible bits and specks. And now and then a bit would drift my way and because it had left the beam of light it swam in I lost sight of it. But I knew, I suspected, no, I knew, it continued its travel until it met the fabric of my cardigan, or the bald spot on my head, or the cuff of my trouser leg. Now the invisible motes, the motes of motes, if you will, were falling all around, everywhere, and all the time, and did not need the sunlight beams to verify them. I trusted they were there. I knew they were. I had faith. You had to. And after about twenty minutes, despite the bass thud thud coming up from Alan below me, I realised I was fully at work. I was undertaking the duties of a Dust Collector. I was earning my corn.

I had placed each day's payment of forty quid in a separate envelope, and made a promise that I would only release it if I had done the work. Any hours I missed, or only half-heartedly undertook (like getting up and losing dust or not caring whether I was truly collecting or not, laughing up my sleeve, i.e. one of any number of species of cynicism), I would return that portion of cash to the lady, or to Harry, if he came along the following Tuesday.

To cut it short, because time is money, as we all know, I did the first two hours like falling off a log. I zipped through it. And I got up, gave myself a good doggy shake, as the lady had suggested, and I took up the envelope with two twenties in it, took out the notes, and felt for the first time in a very long time that I was a working man, a man deserving of respect. Not respect from others, sod *them*, but self-respect, from the truest core of my own existence.

I went into the lounge, which was also my bedroom, and I picked up the phone and dialled the number for The Jade Curtain. It was worth a celebration, don't you agree? Thirty minutes later, as good as their word, their Polish delivery guy rang my bell and handed over four cartons of the good hot food. I even gave him a quid tip.

iv

I repeated my duties up until and including Friday. Two hours each afternoon. It got easier, if anything. When I stopped and shook the dust from my form, I was refreshed, not weighed down and desiccated, like I'd been after any previous work I'd sold my human time for. This was not drudgery, friend, it was a profession. A niche.

I trousered the money and treated myself to a trip to the seaside over the weekend, staying at a little B. & B. I'd stayed in when I was a much happier man, ooh, some twenty years ago. I went to a Korean prostitute the first night for a blow job. She was like a doll. There was a lever at the back of her neck which you could slide and her hair grew or shortened, depending on what way you slid it. I didn't touch the lever, but she demonstrated. You could also press her midriff and she would say things. Hand-me-down phrases that still kept a vestige of their aboriginal honesty. Then I had fish and chips on the beach. It rained a bit. I chucked some chips to a gull. It never said thanks. I went to a pub in the evening and got chatted up by a bald bloke with a pointed beard and tight leather-look trousers. I gave him short shrift.

I met the woman again in The Green Fish the following Tuesday, as we'd arranged. I was glowing with pride and a sense of purpose. 'I can do four hours a day, no worries,' I told her. I looked over at the fire and noticed the dog's metal bowl full of biscuits on the tiles. There was no dog about.

She gave me the serious face. 'Go easy, Mr Tripp. It's all pansies and buttercups at first, but when you extend your hours too quickly, things can happen. The mind...' she tapped her temple with a fingernail, which I noticed was less than clean.

'I was born for this,' I told her, digging into a packet of spicy nuts. 'By the way, where's Harry? Am I ever going to get to meet him? How long have you been his secretary? Why...?'

'Hold your donkeys,' Mr Tripp. 'Which question to you want me to answer?'

I told her I was sorry, that I was just excited, what with this new lease of life, this new found confidence in my ability to generate income, be of some use in the world.

She told me she was not anyone's secretary, rather she was Harry's former wife, and they'd remained friends, despite his starting up with a much younger woman. He'd come into money late in life, and one night when he was in India on a retreat, the concept of collecting dust had come to him in a vision. He told no one at first, but had burnt himself out doing it, and so, eventually, others were needed, conscientious ones, the true soft-working ones, those normally jettisoned by the ignorant beasts of commerce and trade. Those disparaged by the profit monsters, the efficiency freaks. In short, the princes and princesses of uselessness. They were the most useful for such heartwork, for they had lost all pride, had singed their own spirit to such an extent, that to collect dust, and to do this simple act well and with grace, would seem to them the pinnacle of their live's achievements. But they sometimes had to be finessed into recognition of such a curious trade.

My gob must have dropped open. 'So, Harry thinks I'm useless?'

'No person should be used for use,' said the woman, flicking crumbs from the table to the floor. 'It's the highest praise he could bestow upon a person.'

She brought out a buff envelope, which I could see had notes inside. She pushed it over to me. 'Eighty pounds a day for four hours a day, times four days, equals three-hundred and twenty, on the nose.'

'How did you know I'd be ready for more?' I asked.

She pulled her bag apart and showed me a range of envelopes in a neat frill. 'I just chose the one that matched your ambition,' she said.

I turned round and the barman was looking over. 'Is he alright?' I asked the woman.

'He's a collector, too. But he's on sabbatical.'

'And you?'

She looked off, a bit dreamily, 'No...no, I'm much too wilful for this type of work. I'm more of a procurer, so to speak.'

I told her I didn't know that word, and she explained like she was talking to a little boy. I snatched up the envelope and looked inside. What I felt then was disgust mixed with a desire to laugh, or roar like some big animal. 'Monopoly money,' I said to her. 'This is pretend money.'

'It's a pretend job,' she said. 'The purpose is to sink into a profounder truth through the surface of a game. All jobs are games, but their games pretend that they are not games. We need to be unashamed of the game.'

'But you paid me last time, you valued my time,' I said. Getting hotter I was.

'It's an experiment, Mr Tripp, for the world and for your soul. And it will lead you to a place of peace, and your belief will, in time, reverberate minutely across the oceans and the five lands and touch every living person, every wild creature, every coloured leaf, like the tiniest grain of dust touches you - here.' She placed a finger at the centre of her forehead. 'To become supremely useless. To embrace your calling magnificently. Now that would be a very fine thing, don't you agree?'

I looked at the barman again. His head was in his hands like one of them monkeys. Then I turned back. 'But he's got a normal job as well, it gives him some kind of identity, despite the struggle. How can I convince myself of the value of my time if I'm doing pretend things for a pretend reward?' Tears were coming again, and I didn't mind this time. Her face was growing ever more kind, more like a mother sheep and more like a blanket.

She stood and moved to me and brought my face into her bosom. It reeked of old wine. 'But you, my dear, my dearest dear. You have the purity most could never dream of.'

I tried to speak but could only make baby sounds. And I knew then that I would take the pretend money and put in my four hours a day. Become a soldier of uselessness. That I would do it to my utmost inability. Never stinting. Always true. That I had indeed found a rare road to becoming something like I was meant to be.

AS LINDA WAS BUYING THE TULIPS

SARAH DOBBS

My mother twitched with sex. It's the only way to describe it. She'd drift by a man and he would itch, crackle with static. Women feigned oblivion. No one stops to think about that, what that must be like. For your only closeness to be of the body. Her career, friends; they were all a result of her external self. Or so she'd tell me the nights I waited for her step, finished with homework. Her fingers would comb through my hair, nails creating shivers on my scalp. Merlot stained the commas of dry skin on her bottom lip as she closed her eyes and murmured to Joni Mitchell. The hiss and warmth of vinyl like cashmere over the brute roar of the city, a scabbed roasting tin and strained mugs in our sink soaking up the afterglow of her night.

I have painted my mother for more hours than I have masturbated, but I'll never capture that: the sex.

She didn't come to my wedding.

'So we're here, huh? Genital Stage. Better late than never,' she'd said, in an accent people told me was arresting. It emanated from the stage-dark, her having managed to find the moon's spotlight from our old apartment window. The same way a cat will find all the warm spots.

'What?' She looked like Jane Greer.

'My boy.' The creak of a thick page turning in a laminated album.

My wife, herself a good (but not great) artist, gave me three years. It was more than I'd expected. She'd been half in love with my mother – we all wanted something from her, I supposed. My wife became a dandelion. Would find me at night, stippling salmon highlights atop the Prussian blue of my mother's girlish breasts. Stingy things, the chicken-wire check of her ribs easily etched through the softness. I would be lost, trying to replicate the colours within her skin. The shape of leaves in later years, her breasts looked away from each other, and from me. My wife would slip from my studio (she told me this much later). It was also how she left our home, as if blown.

Since, girlfriends have milled, legs and lips. All flimsy, irradiated by my mother's stoic confidence. As they shrank, I spotted them as if from a distance, until losing sight of them altogether. Mother regarded them all with barely a raised eyebrow, ineffective strangers in the crowd of her life, turning instead to trade arms around the waist of another young dancer, another crotch.

Neither of us expected Linda.

*

The dryer spun and bumped, a zip catching and clanging. I met her in the spring. Was staring out the window between where the dryers ended and the washers started. A couple marched down 4th Street in matching orange hoodies and some emblem I couldn't decipher that I presumed gave them that rosy sense of belonging. The man stopped. I cringed as he plucked a single tulip from an outside table, disappearing to pay (I presumed) before handing it to the woman (miming embarrassment) with a magician's flourish.

I hadn't ever thought Linda saw that.

At first I could just feel her as a scent. Spicy and cloying, fried pepper and musk. So overpowering she almost made my eyes water. Turning away from my tumbling clothes, I looked her way, expecting her to be watching me. But her neck was turned to the old man who stood midway down the moaning bank of washers. His left hand up at his ear, he rubbed his fingers together as if trying to rid them of something sticky.

When she turned to me, she folded her arms like a sash across her body. Hip dipped. I would later notice her fire-hydrant hair, the copper skin and that her Matisse-like figure possessed breasts like full bowls of fine sugar. But even the rash of colours she was wearing didn't register at first. It was her mouth that had all the attitude.

Her mouth looked at me, top lip pushing out and up to reveal tiny teeth. Her mouth said, how weird is that dude? and – yeah, you're all right. It did this first with the sneering 'M' shape of her top lip. And with the way she put both together when she really took me in, slowly. Full stop.

*

Linda rattled as we kissed and slipped and gripped in the loos of the laundromat.

'Try – no, here. Yeah. *Ow!*'

'Okay.'

'I – ahhh.'

Her beads clattered against her bowl-like breasts. After, she laughed into my neck, breath smelling of cherry gum and cum. A horror-movie creak as someone, maybe the crazy guy, came in for a piss. Rustle, flush. Didn't wash their hands. I shivered, the sweat cooling on the backs of my knees. Knees that were breaking (she was heavier than the women I usually dated).

I found Linda's mouth mesmeric, as she slung off me like some sheriff, leg peeling from my thighs. Always open, tiny teeth tiled into pink gums. She swallowed, molars biting, mouth still open. Then her mouth shrugged, ticked up at the corner. Maybe it was a smile. I watched Linda walk away, bands of red on the backs of her legs below her indigo skirt. She had a birth mark on her right calf the shape of Italy. The inside of her knees glistened.

*

Whenever I got home, even though that was now not with my mother (I'd tried to put a distance between us) I shuffled in. Would poke my head through the door and peer. I'd expect an image I should look away from. Entering my brownstone in Gowanus, I reminded myself that my mother wouldn't be inside doing pliés and entrechat in the nude, legs scissoring as though scything something up in jealousy. Or be fucking some dancer or model the same age as me. Some pretty faced man-boy with an inhuman body who would roll a smile and ask if I wanted to share a joint.

'My boy doesn't drink,' my mother would say, glancing over her shoulder as she fucked him on our sofa. Somehow, it was worse when she didn't look, and I'd just see the hand clasping her buttocks, skin dimpled in five places so I thought of bowling balls. She squeaked like a mouse when she came.

But by then I'd be in my room, trying to get a record on in time. Sometimes I'd manage, but still I'd hear that little squeak in my ear, as if right next to me. Face hot, I'd wank to thoughts of my kicking her until her stomach, solid as a plank of mahogany, splintered inwards.

When they'd gone, mother was soft and brittle. An open E on a bass guitar, strummed and left to wane. She'd stare into the night from the kitchen window, heavy with an emotion I could never define, moonlight smoothing over her cheekbones, creating sinks of shadow.

I flicked on my floor light. Various parts of my mother's body lined the hallway. I always enjoyed the feeling of walking by them, one eye watching me go.

Linda had scratched her number in two places. The first half was with her nail on my shoulder.

'You're insane, aren't you?'

'Or you've just lived a sheltered life?'

I laughed.

The rest she scratched over a photograph of my mother she'd found in my wallet. My mother had given it to me – a black and white publicity still. Taken before she'd moved, more and more, into choreography and teaching. Lovers usually gushed about how beautiful my mother was. Linda simply removed the square and curled white scars over my mother's face. I had a semi.

'Which comes first?' I'd hooked a thumb to my back.

She'd shrugged, adjusting her clothes. The bra twanged against her back. Little soufflés of skin flowering from either side the strap.

'Wait –'

'Find me.'

'How'm I supposed to know the right combination?'

'Find me.'

With the aid of a mirror I jotted all the numbers on the corner of February's Harper's Bazaar, left by the last girlfriend a couple of months prior.

Come November, I'd just gotten rid of a girl who covered her mouth like a Japanese girl when she tittered and asked if scrambled eggs were used in the military for, like, codes. If it was a joke it was quite possibly funny. But when I asked, she cocked her head.

I made a strong coffee and sat on the settee, an old piece from when they closed down the Rio. It's faded gilt edges, ostentatious claret velour and attic scent gave me a total hard on.

'Such self conscious construction of identity,' mother had

said, when once she managed to leave Inwood and inspect the light in my apartment-slash-studio. Her fingertips had trailed over my jaw, nails catching a cut I'd made while shaving. Heels like a coconut clapping over my Pollack-speckled floor. She'd picked up an acid-yellow pair of thongs with the end of a paintbrush, sent them sailing at me. Left with a tickle at my waist.

'Make sure you eat. You're not a dancer, my boy, your body doesn't need to look like ours.'

It took some trial and error to get the right combination.

'Linda?'

'Did you know a lunar eclipse can only occur when the earth, moon and sun are in syzygy?'

'Siz . . .?'

'Yoked together.'

*

I didn't do the things with Linda that I'd done with other women. She didn't do coke and she didn't get wasted.

'What do you get high on then?'

We'd been watching the eclipse from the roof. Linda sent me a look, which may as well have been her sliding onto my cock. But she was at my feet, me on a stool, swaddled in a duvet. Picking up a parsley crisp she'd baked before coming over, she arrowed it into my mouth. I bit, before the whole thing could be forced down my throat. Didn't exactly go with the port.

Turning to where the stars should be she sucked cheese off all her fingers. Wound up her hair as though tying a ship knot and fastened it with a black scrunchie, beads clacking.

'You just can't do it justice. There'd be almost no point trying to paint it,' I said.

'Ehh,' She shrugged.

I nodded at the sky.

'Oh.'

'Doesn't get you off, I guess?'

'Shall we get some frozen yogurt and watch Doris Day movies?'

I stared at her. 'Let me paint you.' Most women loved this.

'Never.' She stared to where the halo of the full moon could just be glimpsed. It might have been the port. I fixed on the light, thinking about how I could paint it. And then I thought about how all the answers to everything were in that light, but I'd always be fishing as to what the question. I looked at my glass, put it down. Winced, as it scratched on the brick.

*

Maybe it was because I couldn't work Linda out. She was older than me and worked with adopted kids, teased me with talk of threesomes that would never happen (not exactly), her fingers playing over my cock at night, all her plastic rings adding a curious pleasure. Artificial light spilled into our bed from the city, cut with the swoop of headlights, the rattle of night trains, whoops of couples and the late twenties/early thirties clattering home. Sometimes we'd watch the Asian girl and her bouncer boyfriend screwing across the way and then give them our own show. They started to close the blinds. I think we recognised each other in the queue for the bagel cart on one of those crisp bright-blinking Sunday mornings. Her sniffing a balled up tissue leaking cloves, him laden with bags from Forever 21.

*

Linda hung the pictures of my mother along the hallway and I stopped drawing my mother's breasts. I took more commissions, and the life left me a little. I was painting *things*, not spirit. I had Linda. Linda who winked at me like she was in a porn movie when she left every morning, who clipped coupons and made me drink a glass of milk a day, drew our names in caramel or mocha or cappuccino-frost lipstick on all the trees and under all the restaurant tables we ate at. We're everywhere in micro. The last set of our initials was stamped on the side door to the Free Methodist Church on Main Street. Since, on wet days, I've imagined rain bubbling over the letters, just a matter of time till the grease gave out. But I'd caught myself thinking of meandering into old age with Linda. One day, I'd been sure, I would paint the deepening lines aside her mouth, catch all her circus hues in some Fauvist reinterpretation. But I would wake, ribs clenched and sore, after dreaming a shadowy figure had sawed off all my fingers, one by one.

*

In the first six months of Linda, my mother and I had not spoken. But I could feel her focussed disinterest; she would not be the first to break our silence.

'Why not? D'you hate her?' Linda asked one Sunday, handing me dishes to dry.

'Course not.'

She flicked suds at me. 'Fraid she'll hate me?'

I laughed.

Linda slipped her damp hands around my waist from behind. 'She'll love me. Premonition.'

'You'll give me a blow-job after brunch. Premonition.' I unhooked her arms like a seatbelt and walked out onto the balcony for a cigarette. It made a blistering sound as I sucked at it.

*

I sketched Linda one night while she was asleep. Hot and restless – the loft was always polar so we slept in sediments of blankets and invariably woke with the sweat peeling off my skin. I freed my legs from the blankets and pulled up an A5 sketch pad. Her mouth puckered forward like a baby seeking a dummy. The frantic itch of my pencil must have woken her. With one eye winked shut, her forehead lined like screwed up tissue paper, she slapped a hand out. Tearing.

It was heavy weight (165gsm) so she had to chew hard.

Horror bloated me, like those tea flowers women like that bloom in hot water, smearing your glass like an octopus. That was *fucked up*.

When she reached for my hip, brought me to her and I followed the paper down, thinking of my cum softening the fragments inside her, paper with the backwards S of her ear, the bow of her lip, I wanted to pull back.

Linda slept, pieces of us inside her throat.

I sat awake the rest of the night, heartbeat arrhythmic, listening to the building buzzing and flushing and groaning elsewhere, and the light outside turning steadily up until it tickled Linda awake.

She placed kisses across my creased stomach. Climbed over me and thumped naked to the kitchen.

'You want pancakes?'

I scooched down into the pillows, tiredness ironing over me. My commission was due in a week.

'Oh,' she said, appearing from the kitchen with a wooden spoon in one hand and a glass bowl against her stomach, skin gleaming a jaundiced yellow through it. 'Thought I'd meet your mom today.'

Women meeting my mother generally forecast the end of things.

'Sure,' I said, feeling by body unknit and become awash with sleep.

'So I'll call her?'

I opened one eye.

'Found her number in that little blue book of yours. Crossed out Misty and Christy while I was at it. You freaking out yet, hombre?' Out of sight in the kitchen, I heard her Marge-Simpson-chuckle scratch her throat. Could imagine her mouth open as she clawed in air, tongue circling one incisor. 'Hm. There *were* blueberries in here.'

*

The room I used as a studio, a tub of autumn yellow. Yellows in November were richer than summer; browned, deep-fried, thick. Fleeting. I've stood like a zombie for the best part of an hour, bare feet cold against icy throw sheets, watched this yellow turn up and down at least twice, cooled with sudden rain.

I regarded the commission. A monstrous 360 by 270 for a new media firm in the new-hip part of Brooklyn. Their brief was vague: *something autumnal, we want seasonal walls, we want our clients to walk in and feel like it's fall* inside. *We know your work. We trust you.* Problematic, when clients don't write a brief, and then decide they don't quite like what they didn't quite ask for.

I'd put out a palette, was using burnt umber to darken the cadmium yellow (the blues and reds in various blacks would just dull the yellow). I thought of my mother's breasts. Their leaf shape, their inability to meet. The physical distance her own body has for itself.

'Get fucking over yourself,' I muttered. My breath clouded.

'Stopped obsessing over your mother's tits, then.' My mother had crept through the studio in ballet flats. She'd dyed her brown hair blonde. It looked ghostly. Perched just behind my shoulder, she was regarding my commission with that buttery look of amusement she wore just for me. The blonde didn't match her skin-tone; I couldn't place why. It was too pale for the pinks in her skin, or her dark eyebrows betrayed it. But as usual, the overall effect was magnetic. The blonde hair, seemingly unconsidered, waved half-heartedly, girlish. Her body was girlish too. Held with a dancer's assurance.

'I've got it. It's a bird?'

Her clipped accent, South African, always enchanted

people. Far less prominent than when I was a boy, I liked to put it back to how I remembered, in our first apartment in Tribeca. 'Stopped' became 'stupped', 'then' was 'thin'. Everything about her, an interpretation.

'Well well, she must be something special.'

And my brain went: *will will, she mast be samthing spishl.*

'Didn't hear you come in.'

She made a sound like a sleeping cat when disturbed. 'Try locking your door.' Her scent folded into me, sweet talc and fresh flowers. A kiss hit the edge of my mouth. I licked the corner as she arced away; her saliva tasted of peaches.

'I'll make food, you paint.'

The brittleness of this morning's tiredness left me, replaced by something quicker. Irritable need. Absorbed by the maths of colour, time steamed away.

It was the singing that returned me, eyes bulging in the grey. I glanced outside; little eyes all over the city. Amber, red, white.

Singing? No, laughter. Two-toned voices, my mother's dry but light. Invigorated in the way it is when she's usually talking about or with a man, a routine, or what some critic has said of her performances. The less she danced, these were increasingly reflective, name-dropped about the state of dance today. Linda's voice was deeper, but quick to rise. The full range of a piano; moaning and plinking. The dunnnnnnnn of a horror soundtrack from an old Nosferatu maybe, to trills of amazement: *Noooooooo. You're* kid*ding?!*

My mother's sound provided the perfect canvas to Linda. The first time I'd ever thought of her as the backdrop. Even, regular.

The kitchen was a moist well of cinnamon and apricot.

Silence when they caught me watching. Beads of water drip-dripped into the slow cooker. A tagine.

Mother had assembled herself at the kitchen table, Linda by the kettle. Her breasts were gorgeous, thrusting out of a brown wrap dress with exclamatory orange circles. Her white beads, sedate today, sat between the fullness of those breasts.

It was clear, from their briefly exchanged glances, that I'd interrupted. Linda pressed her mouth together so I couldn't read it, which made her tomato lipstick look darker. A shy glance down, her eyelids a tribal tangerine.

My mother leaned her chin on one hand, fingertips tapping her bottom lip. Her entire body yawned sideways. 'Well, well. Mr Bacon has emerged.'

Linda giggled. She knew nothing about art and would not have got the jibe.

My mother straightened, mouth almost pouting, then twisting to the right. 'Have you any lemon?'

*

'So he's a good lover? I raised him to be considerate to women, at the very least.'

'Ah. Well. He doesn't disappoint. You did a wonderful job. Actually, he does this – no!' Linda covered her face with her hands.

My balls flashed hot with sweat. 'Pass the crème fraiche, mother.'

A tambourine-crash of cutlery. The both of them giggled and a feeling corkscrewed into my gut.

*

There was warmth in the loft that December. My women shopped together and went to cafés and analysed independent movies, waking up the apartment with talk of the latest bleak but whimsical Argentinian fantasy. They arrived with packages and draped things across each other and marvelled. They sipped gin in my mother's favourite piano bars and Linda dragged her to underground salsa clubs and they spun together.

'She's fine,' Linda said, when I asked what she thought of my mother. She was straddling my back, massaging my shoulders. Her pubic hair scratched.

'Such a firecracker,' my mother said, sewing a cigarette in and out of her mouth, thumb stroking her throat as she stared at the peppery damp on my ceiling.

*

'So fuck me,' she said.

I was in the studio on a Sunday, the weekend before Christmas. She pulled off her blouse, her beads (wooden today), noosed over her left breast. The nipple was a colour between dried cranberries and chocolate mousse. She stood there, arms out, thumbnail flicking at one of her fingernails. I flashed on the man in the laudromat, thought about a once-loved song fading out, as we both waited for it to stop.

'Let me paint you?' But I was staring at my brushes, checked one against my cheek.

'Never.'

I turned to my winter palette, decaying a pure Prussian with Mars black. It sounded sticky, like when I still used to finger Linda under her bag on the underground. At the edge of my vision, I could see the Christmas lights on the building across the way – a Santa face, three *Ho Ho Hos* streaming from his white beard, each blinking red in turn.

*

Linda began to exist in a parallel universe. I recognised the process; this was how people tidied themselves away. Peeling apart from me like tape.

'Why did your wife leave?'

I was pissing with the door open and resisted the temptation to kick it shut. Maybe Linda wasn't going to be like the others. Maybe she wouldn't fade to black like one of my mother's stages. I zipped, flushed.

If anything, Linda had put on weight, but everything else remained the same. That evening, I will always remember, she looked like a mosaic. Twinkie-yellow cord skirt, aubergine top, one arm packed with gold bangles two thirds of the way up. When she unhooked one Indian-style earring (lime and gold, like a sweet wrapper) scratched at the hole and replaced it, it sounded like someone was playing triangles on her. Her spreading middle was caught by a garnet belt and Majorca-blue highlighted her tawny eyes. As she blinked at me, I thought of an owl, her mouth – *that* mouth – the most alarming marshmallow pink. Saying nothing.

I had a sudden desire to rip her footless tights. The slight extra weight, now I'd noticed it, made the shading of her cheeks that more delicate, the light glossing the apples in a surer point.

'Let me paint you?'

'A question with a question?'

'Can you hear yourself?'

'Can you hear *your*self?'

'Fuck off.' I chastised myself in a silence that seemed to climb in pitch.

'This Mummy's boy shit?' Her mouth pointed at me, curling its disgust. 'Yeah, I said it.'

I flashed ten with my fingers, walked by her.

She cuffed my wrist. 'Oh no you fucking *don't*.'

'You need to leave, Linda.'

She belted me. 'Like that, wouldn't you?'

I wondered what shade of raspberry my cheek would be turning. Tried to walk away.

She pushed me into the wall.

'What the *fuck*?'

We wrestled, me trying to leave, her trying to hold me.

'Do you actually want me to hit you? Really?'

'Make colours on my skin?'

'You know what ...?' I shook my head, broke away. Sighed

and turned back, expecting tears. Some form of begging at least. Right? But Linda stood with her hands on her hips, mouth thrust out as she tongued her front teeth.

The desire to snap a photograph just to defy her, to paint the fucking shit out of her when she was gone, clenched. 'L – ' I'd been stepping towards her.

'You know, your pretty face and 'hip' commissions are gonna take you to late thirties, early forties, tops. After then, what? It'll be tragic. You wanna paint fucking sunshine the rest of your life? Be my guest. But at some point, Jonny – *Jonny* – are you listening?' She shook her head. 'You're gonna have to grow up.'

I narrowed my eyes. 'What?'

She shook her head.

'What?'

'You don't fucking love like this and then make me a ghost of me when you decide. Because, what? You're not good at it, or something.'

'What're you talking about? Lin.'

'*I* know what to do.' Her mouth thinned, decided.

I shook my head.

'Your mom is *wonderful* and you can't stand it, can you? I get it. You don't even know which way you're supposed to love her. Jesus. How fucked up can you get and the thing is – I get it. We'd all be screwed if we'd had to grow up watching our mother fucking guys the age of her *son* –'

'Right –'

'Don't.'

I hung my head up to the ceiling. Straightened. 'Leave, Linda. Now.'

She shrugged. Her mouth gaped. 'No.'

'Are you insane? I don't – *want* – you.'

'Yeah you do. And you wanted a million other maybe-women and they wanted you too. But they left, didn't they. Guess why, genius? There'll always be someone you want more. You know it.'

'You know there's no one else –'

'Your mother, John.'

'Get your fucking shit –'

'John, your mother.'

I saw myself pouncing, hands twisting her throat, but then I imagined Linda and her mouth, both staring levelly back. Completely unaffected. Judging.

'You're going to grow up, John. I'm going to make you.'

I hung, I think, waiting. As so many women had waited for me, before dwindling into the eaves.

'You can't have her, Johnny.' Linda's mouth gave its only ever fake smile. 'I can.'

When Linda left, I felt as though someone had pushed back my head and thinned me down with turps.

*

'So you're an artist?'

The cute brunette (in that organic, Katie Holmes kind of way) twirled a spoon in her chocolate and sucked the tip. Her eyes were a little too wide as she said 'artist'.

We were (optimistically) in an outdoor café. It was spring again, but the weather was still a little too shrill not to hunch. I smoked, hunched, blowing away from her. It buffeted back and she waved, smiling right up into her cheeks to show how brave she was.

My gaze travelled down the street. Linda had drawn a hopscotch down a street like this. Only it was in a neighbourhood where the rents were half the price. Where? Carroll Gardens? It bothered me I couldn't remember. Never drunk, she'd still nicked an empty Bud off someone's steps, smashed it (tidied the glass away) and then scratched an abbreviated hopscotch into the side-walk. I thought I'd fractured my arm when we ended in a heap at 2am, cop lights whisking at the fringes of the night.

In this neighbourhood every other store was organic or

health or zero fat this and that. The one resolute Turkish shop sold stuff from the farmer's market – outside. Tulips and squash, that sort of thing. You could get great cherry chocolate halva from that grocers.

'What do you paint? I took some classes in school – would love a few more lessons. I'm a good student.' She flicked an eyebrow.

The attempt at seduction was cute but inevitably put me off. This girl, with her blazer and polite neckerchief, her little satchel. I thought of the trysts Linda and I had gotten into, how she'd known almost all of the most disgusting things I'd ever contemplated, and still loved me.

'Do you paint things like the seasons? I'd love to be able to do justice to a sunny day like this.'

'Do I fuck paint the sunshine.'

'Oh.'

When I saw them, I knew of course, despite nothing from either of them in the intervening months. Because of course it was heralded in the papers. Linda's disdainful top lip in pixellated black and white, her flea-market eccentricity against the Jackie-O, shades of camel that was my mother. But I'd never actually seen them together myself.

It felt like someone was sucking my face, whooping out all the air. Felt my ass tingle due to lack of oxygen. Or panic. My mother, right there, with a casual yet protecting hand to Linda's back. Finally, at fifty-fucking-something, she'd outgrown her role as the naïveté. My mother and my lover.

Though I was sure she'd seen me, I imagined my mother pressing an internal button that raised her tainted windows. They moved from the grocers with spring onions, balls of something in brown bags, and a skinny bunch of tulips. Linda and her sweet potato skin, her magenta hair, wet with curl gel, lips the colour of the Nevada desert. She lifted a lilac tulip from her bouquet. Her gaze crossed the yard or so to me and she placed the flower down next to the buckets of other tulips before joining my mother.

'I mean, it's like, how can you ever paint something as awesome as the sky? I don't think I'm ever gonna be good enough to capture that kind of beauty.'

'Excuse me.'

I stood and retrieved the flower, watching Linda and my mother shrink. Linda was a shaken bottle of pink champagne, frothing down the street. My mother, proud it seemed, hands in jeans pockets, content to listen. Even from this distance, I could tell my mother was letting the silver populate her restored brunette. The touch my mother then placed on Linda's stomach, round as the full bowls of her breasts, was incandescent with love.

*

We could have all left it at that.

I was painting the mire of shit Linda had left me with. She'd done that for me at least. Weaned me off obsessively pencilling the areola of my mother's tits and shitting out commissions that were the equivalent of cookie cutter Christmas cards. That was gift enough. But then I saw the hand on that belly. Saw it in my dreams, whenever I closed my eyes, like I'd been staring at the sun too long and was dripping light everywhere. Over the weeks, the eventual month, I saw that stomach rising, filling.

Her voice, through the phone connection, was like warm chestnuts.

'There's an end of summer fireworks party. Find me.'

She hung up.

Golden dandelions and the crowd full of *oohs* and *awwws* and then, hearing and feeling embarrassed at their collective response, laughing. No Linda.

I called again.

'There's an autumn proms. Find me.'

Brahms played through the night for lovers and families, the bubble of conversation and heads balanced together in quiet, gelling emotion.

No Linda.

I knocked and the door swung back.

It was like walking through a tunnel. Footsteps in my ears and the *tish* of muted music in the lounge. The soulful roll of a woman's voice: Nina Simone. A slightly acrid burning, tinged with sweetness, a red smell. Incense. It coloured the deeper scent of recent cooking; tomatoes and spices. Unlike my boyhood memories of home, the place wasn't strewn with thighs and quads and pecs. I stepped over a scribble of flesh-coloured tights, shimmering faintly in the dim light, reminding me of snake skin. The thought of what I might find behind the lounge door did not get me hard, as some of my worst dreams over these months had. My pants cold and sticky, threesomes and blowjobs and the taste … I shook my head.

'Hello?'

Cashmere-soft laughter and Linda's giggle threaded over it, like sequins.

'Hello?'

The door was warm to touch. As I pushed, the rose of the fire twitched on vanilla walls. My mother was sewing and looked to Linda when I entered, sucking on a needle which winked in the light. Her neck was bare, thin as a furred pipe cleaner, a tail of hair drawn around to the side of her away from me. Her top lip, as she sucked, a faint frill of lines.

Reaching, Linda turning down the dum-de-dum of Nina so she was just a rumour. There were dinner plates, white crescents swathed out of a rich red sauce by teeth-marked cobs of bread.

'Tonight is the vernal equinox. We're having sparklers on the balcony.'

'Is it mine?'

'I'll leave you two.'

It flooded up, the anger. But my mother's touch on my shoulder kept me in place. Pollen and nectar, her tulip scent, clung to my skin. I wanted to reach up and pincer it off.

'I'd get up, but –'

'It's difficult now?' I was looking to the table, imagining the life nestling inside her.

Linda blinked. I thought of the eclipse, the white corona of the moon. The answers I thought it might contain and the question I couldn't frame.

'It's mine?

'Is that the question?'

I shook my head. She smiled. Her mouth tasted of flowers and I wondered if this was what my mother tasted like too.

'She's all of ours,' my mother said from behind me.

I looked sharply. My mother had taken out her hair and once I would have thought there was nothing and nobody more beautiful. Her soliloquy. Even now, men looking at my mother would twitch. They would see hints of majesty in her body. She cleared the dishes, padding out; I heard the kitchen tap run. But though they would twitch, my mother was finally still.

When I looked to Linda, her mouth dared my disagreement while it laughed at me.

I never painted Linda.

*

At the Indian Road café, at 600 West 218th Street, as Linda was buying the tulips, I said to my date, before I walked away to pick up the flower, 'then you don't paint the sky, do you?'

I felt her watch me all the way down Indian Road.

TRAFFIC

NICK SWEENEY

The baby was calm by the time Svitlana had finished ironing Yuri's shirts. She marvelled at the silence, until the music started up in the apartment downstairs. The baby resumed his wailing to accompany it.

The music was part of her neighbours the Obuchovskis' stepping-out ritual, and it seemed to Svitlana as if it went on for hours. They drank, thumped feet to the beat as they showered and dressed, shouted down their phones to make arrangements. Svitlana could almost see that slut Obuchovska with her back-combed bird's nest, exaggerating her eyes with mascara in the mirror. They would go out into Kiev, even as it flooded with demonstrators and burned, its streets blocked off by police. They'd drink more, drink heavier, listen to louder music, thump those feet harder, dance. They'd come in at four, put even more music on, shout at each other, throw things, call more friends, or they'd make love loudly, growling and mewing. Svitlana's baby would wake again, and cry again.

That was how it started, Svitlana thought. She remembered doing the hair, listening to the music, at home, in the bars, in

the clubs, doing the mewing and growling; that was the part
that had produced the baby, of course. No more fancy hairdos
for her – no point – and the jewellery, the leather jacket, the
boots, nobody looked at them or cared about them when all
she did was wear them up and down the road to the shops
with the baby. The luscious mommies could dress themselves
up all they liked, go to the gym with the crèche in it, drink
the cappuccinos, kid themselves all they liked that they were
living the life, but they weren't; they were just women who
tended to babies, like her.

And they didn't fool her. They wanted to get rid of their
babies. Just as she did.

*

Svitlana wasn't thinking of murder. She was incapable of
murdering anybody, let alone her own child. No, there was
a much better solution. It was elegant, not pretty. It could
never be pretty when you were thinking of selling your baby
to traffickers, but it wasn't brutal, and it was elegant because
everybody ended up happy: she and Yuri would have their
freedom back – her, mostly – and be in funds again; the
traffickers would be happy with the money they made, and, of
course, the western couple who bought the baby would have
their little dream come true to hug in their arms and dandle
on their knees, and show off to their friends and families.
And, most importantly, the baby would grow up happy in
Germany, Britain, America, even, would be educated, drive a
Cadillac, perhaps be president one day.

Ukraine was imploding in the face of threats by outsiders,
and by its own nationalists, gaping with shortages, hospitals
no good, services gone to ruin, political life reduced to slogans
shouted by stupid men with guns. It had been a mistake to
have a baby in such times – she was twenty two, for heaven's
sake, and Yuri was twenty four. She was too young to be
closeted away all day with nothing to do, and nowhere to

walk the walk and talk the talk and wear the clothes and live the life.

And Yuri still played his football every Friday evening, still did his weightlifting, went for his swims at the pool. He still saw his friends. Okay, he didn't go out for the late-night drinking marathons anymore, and he didn't blow all his pay on the ridiculous stuff that attracted some men, stunted their growth and kept them as boys. In fact, he gave most of it to her. He was a good man; straight in his thinking, and he was courageous, unafraid of standing up for himself, and for her. He was a bore, though. Svitlana wished she could appreciate him as a friend – she wished her father had been like Yuri, wished her lazy brother was like him. She wished she hadn't married him, wished she hadn't had the baby with him.

'This is no place to bring up a child,' she reminded Yuri whenever she could. 'We must change things.'

They could both speak decent English, but it was too ambitious to try to go to Britain or the States. Svitlana also had some Romanian from her four years as a dogsbody at a Moldovan export firm based in Kiev until the crisis. It was not ordinarily a useful language, but Svitlana knew that in Bucharest there was plenty of work in hospitality and catering for her, and plenty for Yuri on the building, and the Romanians were not too strict about foreign workers. It was cheap to live there, and they could save their money, and put it towards heading further west, or coming back to Kiev when the trouble was over. Wasn't it a plan?

Yuri often seemed as if he wasn't listening. 'What about the baby?' he said. He nodded over to him, sleeping, oblivious.

'We're too young for a baby. We are, really.' Svitlana exhausted her list of unsuitable relatives with whom they could leave him, knew from their repetitions of this conversation that Yuri had misgivings about all of them. As ever, she let his own responses fix the drawbacks in his mind. She seemed to be joking when she conjured up untrustworthy Gypsy women who'd pretend to look after him in Bucharest. 'And then sell him to a rich western couple,' she said. And she seemed to be joking again when she said, 'I mean, we could do that.'

Yuri wasn't just a good man. He was clever, too. He saw what Svitlana was getting at.

'And everybody would be happy,' Svitlana joked.

'Everybody.' Yuri seemed to be smiling. 'But poor baby would miss his mama.' Svitlana sketched out a scenario of the baby's life in America; the college, the Cadillac, the run for the White House, made Yuri laugh lightly. 'You need to know the right people,' he warned her. 'And they're hard to find.'

'But not impossible.' Svitlana willed Yuri to make a connection to what she was thinking, but he just gazed at the baby. Finally, she had to prompt him with the words, 'Didn't you meet one of them, once? At the gym?'

'Oh yes. We were talking about our jobs, and he said to me, "And what do you do, then?" And I said, "Pipe fitting. How about you?" and he said, "I'm a baby trafficker."'

She tried to join Yuri in a smile – he was turning it into a footnote to their evening, as if he'd simply told her a joke, or a rambling story about babushkas and drunks. But she hadn't imagined it, had she, the chance meeting in a locker room, and Yuri's reading of the man's expression when talk had turned to work, maybe his hearing a chance remark into the phone as the man dressed, the sight of a jail tattoo that revealed his role to those who knew, or the sight of his car keys, Yuri's seeing a gleaming villain's choice BMW purring off into the night. Had she only imagined that? And why had he even mentioned it?

The baby cried. Yuri picked him up, quieted him. The Obuchovskis' music started up downstairs.

*

Svitlana loved her country – of course she did – but it was strangling itself with its strife. The school across the road had been closed all day, but nobody had been told, parents having angry conversations on phones, kids running wild in the street, up and down in the lifts, on the stairs, gathering in the playground down by the block with its broken, ugly sculptures. Despite their unexpected freedom, the schoolchildren were bored, and malevolent. Svitlana didn't want her baby to grow up to be one of them, on this street, or on any other in Kiev.

There were rumours of two men carrying guns openly at the end of the street. Thugs, anarchists, robbers, nationalists, separatists, police? She didn't know, and then next thing Svitlana heard that the men had gone into the grubby shop on the corner, picked up a packet of kitchen roll, had no change to pay for it – not no money, just no change – and pulled a gun on the shopkeeper when he declared that he in turn had no change, and wouldn't let them have it. So they'd taken their prize like they were James Bond, darting against walls, behind cars, on an urgent mission to wipe up spills.

And the power off the night before for eight hours, like in some Third World hellhole, all the stuff warm in the fridge. And Yuri's bus delayed by queues at fuel stations, people filling their cars full of panic-bought supplies. She loved her country, yes, but it really was time to leave. And then, in a year or two, when it had argued itself hoarse, and when the mouthiest men had been shot by other idiots with guns, and all the blood wiped up with kitchen roll, when sense reigned – a woman in power again, maybe – she and Yuri could come back.

'We can have another baby,' she urged him. 'Later, when we're older. And we'll have more money, and can have a child minder, and can send him to a private school, a proper school, not like that... mental ward across the road. We can have two, a boy and a girl, of course.' She'd laughed loudly, and rather stupidly. It wasn't funny. She was just trying to draw Yuri into the feeling she had, get him to share a breath of the air she was imagining.

'Bucharest?' Yuri was right to scoff. Both of them had been brought up on the idea that anybody with ambition would go to the west. Ten years before, had anybody suggested they go to a place like Bucharest, they would have been laughed out of the room. But nobody believed in that dream of the west anymore, and that could have been good, but instead they believed in homelands, with a savage nationalism or an equally savage separatism.

'For a while. A chance to take a breather. Away from all this trouble here.' They'd had all their troubles, the Romanians, shot their dictators, settled into being a shambolic democracy, but at least it had peace. And there was money there, not millions – unless you counted them in Romanian lei – and there was work, and stability, and nobody was shooting guns. 'Yuri, it's dangerous here, it's… deadly.'

She didn't only mean the men with the guns, the stone throwers, the wreck of the town centre, and of the economy; the picture she saw of herself·up in her tower, staring out the window, the Obuchovskis and their music downstairs, the baby crying – that was just as deadly to a girl of twenty two.

'There's… prosperity there,' she said. 'A girl I know went there said the city centre shops are all western – I mean no Romanian writing on them at all, all the adverts, the billboards, all in English. Crazy, eh? But, you know, people are happy when they're prosperous, Yuri.' And of course she knew that was nonsense, but she was enthused now, anxious not to let the idea of this possible future slip out of his view.

She reached for her laptop, for the page she'd bookmarked, a forum of Ukrainians' comments about places to rent, and about the work there, and how its word-of-mouth system functioned, with pointers to where to go, even who to seek out… She clicked and clicked, saw that the connection was down, looked up, saw a corner of the city dark. She snapped the thing shut, went back to babbling, repeated all the buzzwords, saw Yuri nodding, as if memorising them, his smile on, his phone in his hand.

*

The man looked at the baby. The baby smiled. The man took a deep breath, caught a whiff of baby; an antiseptic smell, not entirely pleasant, though it seemed neither to please nor displease him. He said, 'Good,' and turned to Svitlana.

She and the man studied each other. He was mid-thirties, she thought, handsome in a cruel way – remote, she thought, a man whose thoughts nobody could ever know. Kazak in his eyes – from way back, maybe – Tatar? He wore unremarkable clothes, she saw, but the accessories were the real thing, the watch – Rolex? No, the other one that went for a king's ransom – the rope of gold necklace she could see just under his open shirt collar, the sunglasses in his top pocket. He was the real deal, for sure. You couldn't always tell; the city was full of liars and blaggers, scammers and braggers and, in fact, people who just said the first thing that came into their crazy heads. But there was something in this man's eyes that warned of the lengths to which he would go to make a living.

His eyes were dispassionate, almost disinterested, as they rested on her face, then moved down her body briefly. Svitlana felt herself just a little flattered, found herself sticking her chest out.

'How much are you asking?' the man said.

Svitlana looked at Yuri. He mouthed the sum they'd agreed on. She named it. The man seemed to be thinking about it. Svitlana wasn't fooled by that, was sure he'd already decided what he'd pay. The man said, 'I will consult,' took his phone out and walked into the hall with it, and out the door onto the communal landing.

'You didn't finalise it with him,' Svitlana whispered to Yuri. She kept her eye on the door. 'I thought you'd… discussed it. I thought you'd made an agreement.'

Yuri said, 'These people keep you in a permanent state of negotiation, right till the last minute. That's how it works.'

Svitlana wanted to ask more questions, but it was plain

that nobody would be able to answer them except the man outside the flat. 'That's how it works, then,' she agreed. She felt worldly and businesslike when she said the words. 'It's a buyers' market.'

'What?'

'A buyers' market, Yuri. That's when… when the buyers call all the shots.'

'Oh.' Yuri's expression was half-frown, and half-grin, as if he was holding himself back from a patronising remark. 'No, Svitlana,' he said, choosing a neutral tone that was almost kindly. 'It's not. Neither buyers nor sellers call the shots. The market always belongs to the men in the middle.' He pointed towards the door. 'The men who do the things the buyers and sellers don't have the nerve to do. They call the shots.'

'Good news.' Their man with the nerve was back in their living room, hands in his pockets, something like a smile on his face. He said to Svitlana, 'I am authorised to pay you a little more than your asking price.' Without ceremony, he pulled a wad of notes out of his pocket, and handed it over to Svitlana. 'Count it,' he commanded her.

Dumbfounded, and barely able to contain the mad flush of her good feeling, Svitlana could only look at the money in her hand. She came to her senses and handed it to Yuri, said, 'Yuri, please, you count it. I will only make a mistake.' She giggled, stupidly, invited the men to do so too, if they wanted to. They didn't. 'But what am I thinking of…' Out of the corner of her eye she saw Yuri flicking methodically through the notes. 'Please, you must have a drink with us, to… to celebrate. We have some vodka.'

'No thank you.' The man patted his pocket, made his car keys chink. 'Not while working.'

She remembered suggesting to Yuri that he take the man out for a drink, a week back, ten days, once he'd positively identified the fellow as a trafficker. And Yuri saying, 'These people only drink with their friends. It's their rule.' She looked at Yuri, fearful that he'd detected her *faux pas*, and the look in his eyes told him that he had, but that he forgave her.

'Of course,' she said coldly, as if her invitation to drink had been a mere test of the man who was to drive her baby away, conveying the precious cargo to a safe home, to education, the presidency. She invited him into another staccato laugh. 'Completely correct, and... right.'

'All good?' the man asked Yuri.

'All good,' Yuri replied. He came and put his arm briefly around Svitlana, squeezed her shoulder, passed on, shook the man's hand.

'So, expect a call.'

'Excuse me?' Svitlana spread fingers towards the cot and its tiny occupant, the pile of blankets, the bulging bags full of baby clothes, nappies and soft toys. She thought she'd make the man laugh when she said, 'Don't forget him.'

The man didn't get near a laugh. He said, 'I'm not the baby man. I'm the money man.'

Svitlana had to strain to keep her eyes calm, her expression composed. They needed every last penny of the fee to start their life in Bucharest, of course, but she'd thought it wouldn't have done any harm to have one big night out in Kiev – especially now that the fee had increased. She'd wanted to go through the Obuchovskis' stepping-out ritual; the hair, the lipstick, the perfume, the nails, the clothes, the thump of music, for the pleasure of it, the anticipation. And, while she was at it, to give her neighbours a taste of their own medicine. It had been months since she'd been for a night out.

And, she had to face it, she'd made her goodbyes to the baby; in her mind, he was gone. Having him and the money in the flat together was somehow not right, just not... correct. She said only, 'But...'

Both Yuri and the man waited politely for a few seconds. Svitlana realised that nothing she said was going to change the plan, and that she'd have to save the stepping-out ritual for another time. The man turned to go.

Another thought occurred to Svitlana. 'You don't want to... examine him?' she said. She couldn't put it into words, but surely it wasn't beyond the bounds of belief that people tried to fool traffickers by offloading on them babies who had... problems, a lack of limbs, of fingers, of brain, a strawberry birthmark shaped like a horse's head.

'The baby? The trafficker seemed surprised, then understood, nodded, said, 'I've seen him. Your husband told me all about him, and he is a man of his word, I am sure.'

'Of course,' Yuri said, and Svitlana echoed him, as did the trafficker.

'I'm not... qualified. I'm the money man. You got your money, yes?' It was a jovial question, and the man accompanied it with a jovial face, but still waited for Svitlana to answer. 'So. That's how it works. You'll meet the baby man in the next few days, and then your troubles will be over. The great migration.' He wiggled his fingers. 'Fly away, birds.'

*

Yuri was weighed down with the bags, but strong, uncomplaining. Svitlana was ahead. It had started out as a warm evening, but the night would be cold, and she was glad Yuri had insisted she bring her leather jacket to complement the hair, the nails, the eyelashes, the stepping-out heels.

She giggled. It was strange to be taking the baby out in the dark. She was a little sad. In the two days since the money man had visited, Svitlana had sensed the pull of bonds she'd never dreamed existed between herself and the baby. He was a lovely little man. But the great thing was that all babies were lovely little people. And another great thing was that, some time in the future – five years, maybe, in Romania, maybe, in Britain, maybe, and why not? – she'd have another lovely little man, and a lovely little woman, too, and when that happened, she'd do things properly, build them a good life.

She had started off all wrong with the baby; it wasn't his

fault that he was a little accident in a country on the verge of eating itself up with bitterness and carnage, but at least she'd been able to give him a new start, the start he'd deserved all along. 'Mister President,' she whispered in his ear as she lifted him out of his carriage.

She'd seen the car turn into the street, the dark green SUV they were expecting. From the passenger side, a track-suited young man – he looked even younger than Svitlana – jumped out.

'The baby man.' Svitlana had rehearsed the greeting, and the comic face she put on with it, but neither had the heart-lightening effect she'd envisaged, either on her or the baby man.

He narrowed his eyes, made a scowl that verged on the friendly, did an exaggerated double-take, moving his shoulders, and said, 'You what?' He pulled the rear doors open. The seats had been put down to clear a space for everything, Svitlana saw. She was pleased, and pleased too to be seeing the last of those imperfect little home-made clothes in pastel colours, those nappies, those awful awful toys everybody had bought the baby.

The baby seemed a little alarmed, sensed something going on. He wriggled. He opened his mouth to make an experimental wail. Yuri leaned over, shushed him, made noises that diverted him. 'Give me him,' he said. 'Time to say goodbye.'

Svitlana handed him over. Yuri turned around, cooed urgently at him. Now that Svitlana had let go of him, she was anxious. She took a look round at the baby man.

The gel in the baby man's short, spiky hair gleamed, and he had a tattoo on his neck, and though those were part of a common enough style, it struck Svitlana that she'd never seen such a man taking care of a baby; he didn't look very... qualified to be a baby man. He had a missing front tooth, made it part of a terrible grin. He shoved Svitlana in the chest, and sat her down on the rear part of the car. He stuck a syringe quickly into her neck and pressed the plunger until it was all the way in.

'Comfortable?' the baby man said.

Svitlana knew that there were questions she wanted to ask, but she didn't know what they were. It was easier to nod. The young man lifted her legs gently, and pulled a restraint for a wheelchair out and fixed it around her ankles. He shut the door, and walked round to the passenger side. With a purr of the engine, the car had gone, had merged into the traffic.

Yuri thought the baby was no longer puzzled. He gurgled, and wiggled his fingers. Yuri said, 'Come on, little man. Let's buy us an ice cream. And then we'll have to find you a new mama.'

A TRIP OUT

JUNO BAKER

The plants reach up to a plasterboard sky. Artificial sunshine creates tropical heat. Jim wipes the sweat from his upper lip and caresses the jagged edge of a newly unfurled leaf. He has learnt to be gentle with these creatures, not to crowd them as he gazes at the sinewy veins threading through their foliage and the buds that cluster in their hands. Every day he becomes more skilled as their servant. They have trained him to recognise their wants before they become wanting, and yet they thirst for copper and iron, potash and loam. They hunger for phosphorous, seaweed and bonemeal.

Spider should have been here two days ago with the *Feed 'n' Gro*. Sweat collects in Jim's faded hair as he shakes the bag to loosen the last bits from crinkles in the polythene. 'Profound apologies,' he says, because there aren't any last bits; there weren't any yesterday either. 'Profound apologies. Normal service will be resumed as soon as humanly possible.'

He edges along the cracked wall to the window and hooks a finger round the blanket that shields the plants from the outside world. Every week Spider comes with the *Feed 'n'*

Gro and leaves with the magical harvest, so that its wisdom may be spread in the smoking of amethyst bud. That's the arrangement. But this week Spider is nowhere to be seen. Jim watches the clouds gather above the houses opposite: smart houses these days with sage-green front doors and window boxes full of herbs and crimson geraniums. The street is lined with cars, shiny ones lying in wait for him to make a wrong move.

It wasn't always like this, his street. It used to be full of families and squatters. When he first lived here, boys played football outside his window and the old man opposite would shuffle up to the corner shop in bedroom slippers. It was a happy friendly place before the shiny cars moved in. But that's all changed now, even the corner shop with its organic this and organic that – organic everything Jim needs except for *Feed 'n' Gro*. If they stocked *Feed 'n' Gro* it wouldn't matter when Spider turned up. Jim could sort everything out on his own.

He takes himself off to the kitchen, plonks himself down in front of the telly and smokes amethyst bud to get his head straight. On television a car is driving along empty roads. That's a lie for a start, but most people don't see it. There aren't any empty roads, not anymore. And there's no driver in that car; it drives of its own accord. The cars are in league. Whenever Jim crosses the road they ambush him, which is why he hasn't crossed a road for he doesn't know how long. Usually, he doesn't need to take the risk: he has the corner shop and Spider. But Jim has a nasty feeling the cars may have done for Spider to stop him supplying the plants with *Feed 'n' Gro* – to stop him spreading the magical harvest. If Jim trusted phones he'd ring Spider. Trouble is the cars would listen in, or worse, they'd shoot cancer through the airwaves to grow tumours in his head.

Because the cars have more than one way to finish you off. They can mow you down, turn other machines against you or poison you with pollution. Now that he thinks about it,

Spider wasn't as sprightly as all that when he came round last week. He was wheezing when he arrived and continued to wheeze as he handed Jim the bag of *Feed 'n' Gro*. After he'd sloughed off his anorak, he fell to the chair clutching his chest. Jim remembers the rasp of laboured breathing – In. And Out. In. And Out. 'Just me old ticker giving me gyp,' Spider had said, coughing up phlegm and spraying it over the table.

'Pollution!' Jim had told him, 'Part of the machines' master plan!'

But all he got from Spider was the usual 'Yeah, yeah mate! It's all right.'

*

The plants in Jim's bedroom have begun to wilt and sigh. He's failing them. He feels their heartbreak and disappointment. His attempts to placate them are feeble and unsatisfactory. 'Perhaps a little night music, if our friend Amadeus would oblige?' Usually they love Mozart but today nothing can cheer them. They are weak. They must feed. If Jim doesn't get hold of some *Feed 'n' Gro* soon, the plants will starve. He will have to leave the flat, journey to the high street and find the hardware shop where Spider buys the *Feed 'n' Gro*. He knows the dangers, knows the cars are out to get him and that such a quest is almost certain suicide. He remembers the first time he understood, that night in the squat all those years ago when he and Spider were still young and Spider was still skinny. They used to grow their own then too, but it was just weed, not like the magical harvest they grow now. And they tripped a lot: mushrooms, acid, anything to alter images, open the doors of perception. That's when Jim first saw the ribbons of white from the street lamps interweave with the beams from car headlights. That's when he noticed the cars glaring at him with snide grins. And as the twisting light taunted him, Spider was telling him not to be frightened. 'It's okay mate. Everything's gonna be all right.'

But everything isn't all right because Spider hasn't come.

*

Jim stands on his doorstep under a sullen sky, listening to the murmur of cars on the distant high street. As long as it stays light, he reckons he stands a fighting chance of getting across the roads safely. Seeing as he hasn't been up long it must still be early in the day, so he needn't worry about the dark. He has to cross a couple of roads – his own first. His best bet is to get to the bend by the corner shop, try to cross there. He's no fool; he knows the shiny cars are only pretending to be parked, so he takes his time looking to the left of him, the right of him, the left of him, before creeping out.

Somewhere, a growling roar is rising to a crescendo. He scurries across – glancing this way and that, that way and this. It appears from nowhere, grinning. It's heading straight for him, squealing as he quickens his pace and hobbles faster. He only just makes it, stumbling as he gets to the pavement. Behind him, a human voice shouts 'Bloody idiot!' He hears the car move on and looks down at his broad calloused hands, sees his feet below. Yes, all present and correct. The world around him is as it should be: houses, front doors, window boxes. This is better than expected. The car completely missed. Quite satisfactory. He chuckles to himself and shuffles up the road to the high street.

Now for the big one. There are four lanes of traffic between Jim and the hardware shop. Of course, there's the pedestrian crossing, but how can he trust the little green man? The little green man is embedded in the technology of the traffic lights, the cousins of the Belisha beacons, who, in turn, are distant relatives of the street lamps. There's no doubt about who's on whose side here. If he trusts the little green man's electronic bleats, he could be slain.

At the high street the howling traffic charges in both directions. Flatulent and belching, it seethes forward in a fuming stampede, its foul breath full of particulates and parabens. Time for a think. He could run for it, race across the road trying to dodge cars, but they are faster than him, and there are more of them. Or he can take a chance on the little green man, but he will need to outsmart him. He's in a dither, unsure, and stares down at the kerb.

He's thinking hard when the scuff of shoe on pavement distracts him. White socks in silver-pink trainers skip up beside him. A girl in a pale pink coat presses the button. A woman bustles up beside her, looks Jim over and snatches the child's hand. The woman stares straight ahead; the girl stares at Jim. A man comes – young and restless wearing one of those puffed up coats. Two school boys in uniform barging each other with their bags. An old lady with a dog that sniffs at Jim's crotch. A portly gentleman on a mobile scooter. A crowd is forming.

Jim steps back from the kerb, lets the people surround him. When the green man starts bleeping, he hides among the people, keeps his head down so the cars won't see him. He senses the traffic edging forward and hurries along until somewhere, just after the halfway point, the crowd begins to fall apart. The restless young man veers off to the left. The mobile scooter speeds ahead. The girl and the woman start running, leaving him exposed. The cars edge forward, revving, but he makes it across the road just in time.

Ha! So the cars aren't so clever after all! He can outwit them. For a brief moment he becomes vainglorious, abashed at the thought of a second victory, but then he gathers himself together, reminding himself that it doesn't do to be smug, and squints ahead up the high street. Not far now – a few shops up on the right bold black letters spell 'Dicken's Ironmongery' against an orange background.

The door is solid glass, heavy, and the shop behind it, bigger and darker than it looked from the outside. Jim stands in the doorway blinking, waiting for his eyes to resume normal service. The shopkeeper looks him up and down, taking in his filthy parker and grimy jeans. 'Can I help you?'

Jim knows that he's disgusting to other people. 'Profound

apologies,' he begins, bending a little. 'Perhaps you'd be so kind as to direct me towards the *Feed 'n' Gro?*'

The shopkeeper doesn't move from behind the counter, takes a moment to process the question and answer it. 'Third aisle. Halfway down. Somewhere on the left.'

'Much obliged.' Jim shuffles off to complete his mission. When he finds compost and secateurs he knows he must be in the right area, that soon he'll see what he's looking for. He's doing better than he expected, even feels a little proud. Tonight his plants will feast. He will buy as much *Feed 'n' Gro* as he can carry. After all, he has the money.

When Spider held out the wad of notes last time, it seemed much thicker than usual. Jim's fingers wiggled nervously at the cash.

'Take it – you earned it,' Spider snapped impatiently.

'Well if Sir insists.' Jim blushed. 'Though my work is a vocation I'm honoured to perform.'

'Yeah-yeah, whatever...' rasped Spider, leaning back to squeeze his roll of notes into his tight jeans pocket. 'I dunno, Jim. State I'm in, be a miracle if I get home without dropping dead!'

Jim didn't like the way he'd said that, or the clammy pallor in Spider's skin, or the hoarse cough that bent him double when he got to the front door, but all he said was, 'Just be sure to mind the traffic.'

Perhaps Spider's not well, he thinks. That would explain why he hasn't visited.

As he ruminates, his eyes settle on the words *Feed 'n' Gro*. He grabs as much as he can carry and stumbles back through the shop towards the counter. Clutching five large packets to his chest, he decides now he knows he can outwit the cars, he might visit Spider, look after him for a change. He drops the *Feed 'n' Gro* on the counter. The shopkeeper purses his lips as he bags it up, but Jim's used to being despised – it doesn't worry him. Everything is going swimmingly. The shopkeeper rings it all up, tells Jim what's owed, and Jim passes over the money. All fine.

Until the street lamp snaps on. Jim sees it through the window behind the shopkeeper's head. It glows red, is warming up. But this is all wrong. It's too early to go dark because Jim only woke up a short time ago. His eyes can't provide normal service at night. The cars know this. That's when they blind him with their headlamps. That's when the streetlights cast ribbons of bright neon to confuse him and trip him up.

The shopkeeper says something about change, there on the counter. Jim stares at the street lamp outside. Red is for danger. He'd like to stay in the shop, just for the night, but can't explain this to the shopkeeper. He looks round – he doesn't know why – may be for somewhere to hide, some means of escape. 'Oy!' the shop-keeper bellows, 'Your change. Are you gonna pick it up or what?' His pin eyes fix on Jim as he juts his dented chin towards the heap of change.

Jim doesn't want to go, but the man's stare is so cold, his voice so cranky, that he backs out of the shop. His feet guide him to the pedestrian crossing where his finger presses the button and he waits for other pedestrians. No one comes. The bleats begin, and Jim rushes, his bags heavy with *Feed 'n' Gro*. The plastic handles twist, cutting off the blood supply to his fingers as he glances at the cars, keeps an eye. He spots a bus at the halfway point. The driver smiles one of those sympathetic smiles where the lips disappear. Jim doesn't have to hurry for him – he's a human driver, of a bus too. He smiles back. He would wave if his fingers weren't being strangled by polythene, but all he can do is smile and nod as he hurries past the bus. He doesn't notice the four-by-four edging forward, doesn't know what hits him.

Strings of light knot and tangle above, giddy and excited, passing messages down the line. The bus driver's face looms in underneath them, tells him to lie still. 'It's okay mate. Everything's gonna be all right. Ambulance is on its way.'

But everything is not going to be all right. The plants are

calling for *Feed 'n' Gro*. He can hear them and as his eyelids grow heavy, the squeal in his bedroom grows louder. Who will protect the plants now? It's all his fault. He shouldn't have come out so late.

'Profound apologies, profound apologies,' he whimpers, eyes closing. 'Normal service will be resumed as soon as humanly possible.'

.

A DEBT

DAN COXON

Greg didn't smell the exhaust fumes, or notice the faint thrum of the engine behind the garage door. The package for 3788 Ostler – C. Stein, Mr – was from a company called The DollHaus. It was the third this month. The parcel should require a signature, but unofficial company policy was to knock, then leave it at the door. It was what he'd done before. But when he'd mentioned Mr. Stein to his sister she'd hounded him for details, and he knew she wouldn't let it go.

After knocking – twice, with no response – he peered through the wire mesh of the screen door. That was when he heard the car engine. And, finally, caught the oily scent of exhaust fumes in the air.

Looking back, Greg wasn't sure what he'd expected to find. A car idling while its owner unpacked groceries from the trunk, maybe. Or an amateur mechanic tinkering with the engine. It took him a few seconds to make sense of the foggy interior, then he dropped the box he was carrying. As he tugged the car door open a green snake of garden hose slid out of the window and coiled at his feet. The man inside watched him dozily. He leaned across and yanked out the key, the engine dying. A few seconds later the hose stopped hissing. Mr Stein blinked a few times, his chest spasming like a landed fish as he wheezed some air into his lungs. When he spoke his voice sounded thin.

'Well, that was unexpected,' he said.

*

He found Janice on a bench, looking out over one of the neighbourhood's weedy, pebble-strewn beaches. A Sudoku book was wedged between two slats, her pencil tucked into her hair. The wind and her makeshift hairdo made her look like something intended to ward off seagulls.

'Dolls? What does a grown man want with dolls? You're sure he doesn't have a family?'

Greg couldn't explain it – at least not in a way that would satisfy his sister – but yes, he was sure. He knew that 3727 Ostler had two kids, one in high school, one in day care; 3707 Ostler lived alone, a war veteran with a taste for imported British candies; 3699 Ostler was a qualified architect moonlighting as a fairground psychic on the weekends. He could tell you what brand of doggie vitamins 4777 Beach Drive gave her startled, rat-like Chihuahua, or which Internet site 2980 Pacific bought his gay porn from. Some of this he deduced from labels and delivery manifests. Other times they would share the innermost details of their lives with him on their doorstep, as if he was a doctor or a priest, not a delivery guy with a raw line of chafed skin on his inner thighs. The boxes he handed over were care packages from the real world.

'It's just him. You should see his lawn. Not a blade out of place. And flat. There's no way a kid's set foot on that in the last year.'

'Flowers?'

'None. Just one empty bed at the front, about an inch of bark on top. Like he doesn't want anything to grow there. Ever.

'Hmph.'

He could see Janice looking for how the pieces slotted into place. When they were kids she'd been obsessed with mystery stories, her room stacked with dog-eared copies of *The Hardy Boys*, and *Alfred Hitchcock's Three Investigators*. From an early age she'd always been the one to bring home the neighbourhood strays.

'Definitely sounds like a loner. Which means the boxes are either blow-up sex dolls, or the guy has unresolved issues from his childhood. I'm not sure which I like more.'

'Not sex dolls. Too heavy. And they rattle sometimes, if I shake them. Which, you know, I try not to do... But. There's more in there than just an inflatable Annie.'

'Maybe he's sitting on a Barbie goldmine, then. These things are collectable now, I guess. I wonder who he has in his life. We all need somebody. Someone who isn't seven inches high and made of plastic.'

He could hear her thoughts ticking through the usual motions, trying to fix the stray soul. His sister, the Northwest's answer to Mother Teresa. She never had learned to let these things go. Sometimes he wondered if they were related at all.

*

The paramedics eventually declared Mr Stein fit, but someone had to stay with him for a couple of hours. It was as Greg volunteered that he remembered the parcel. Stein seemed stable but he didn't want to take any chances, so they walked out to the garage together. The paramedics had left the doors open and the sea breeze had dissipated the fumes. A few leaves had blown in, circling the car. Stein stood at his shoulder as he gathered the parcel. One of the corners had been flattened to a rounded curve, the card crumpling in tiny waves. On the adjacent edge there was a split and a white nugget of packing material poked its head out through the torn card. There was a tinkling inside like the sound of a miniature sleigh bell.

'I'm sorry about the state of this. The company has insurance, if you want to make a claim.'

Stein's face was unreadable. After they'd paraded back inside, he placed the damaged box on the dining table and picked at the tape with his fingernail. As one end came free the box collapsed outwards, the damaged seams surrendering. The packing foam spilled like snow across the tabletop. Nestled in the centre of the drift Greg saw a porcelain figure of a man. It was only three inches high, wearing lederhosen and a hat with a feather tucked into the brim. The feather was intact but both the man's legs had snapped off at the knee. He was lying on his side, the splintered shards of his feet and calves spread beneath him. The pink blushes painted on his cheeks reminded Greg of overripe plums.

'I'll get a brush,' Stein said. 'We don't want to cut ourselves.'

After Stein had cleared away the box and its contents, Greg made a few clumsy attempts at conversation. But Stein showed no interest in the football season, or the daily routines of his delivery route. He showed very little interest in anything. The way he kept staring off into space made Greg wonder whether he might already be planning another suicide attempt. In a desperate attempt to distract him he finally asked about the cracked porcelain figure.

'Of course, you'll want to see my collection. So silly of me. I should have offered already. It's what people usually want to see when they come here. Follow me, follow me.'

The small room at the rear of the house was fitted from floor to ceiling with wooden shelves, the shelves spaced a foot apart, the last one exactly a foot from the ceiling. Arrayed around the shelves were figurines like the one Greg had just delivered, packed into every spare inch of space. All looked to be on a Germanic theme, from an alphorn player to a fierce-looking fräulein. Some peered over shoulders. Others were lost in the crush. The effect was dizzying, as if a thousand pairs of eyes were staring at you from every surface.

'Isn't it something? There are Goebel collectors all across

the world, you know. But my collection is considered one of the most complete. Four hundred and fifteen porcelain figures, to be precise. Only fifty-two short of the recognized record, and the largest Hummel Club collection in North America. If I have a legacy then you're looking at it.'

Greg didn't know what to say.

'Usually I don't even let anyone touch them, but you must take one home with you. I insist. It's the least I can do. Any one, your choice.'

Greg stared at the ranked shelves as if they were about to topple onto him. There was no way he could tell Stein that porcelain dolls weren't really his thing. Without thinking he reached for the first figure he saw, a portly gentleman with a black cat curled around his shoulders.

Stein slapped his hands together. 'Excellent choice! That's a vintage piece from the early Sixties, quite remarkable for the facial detail. I knew you would choose well, I just knew it. Now, can I offer you tea? Or coffee?'

There was still almost an hour to kill before his caretaker duty was over, so Greg accepted. As they sat sipping from delicate china cups his eyes drifted back to the figurine, the gentleman's eyes smirking at him through the layers of varnish. There was something unnervingly familiar about it. Maybe it was the glazed expression on its face. Blank, like Stein's.

When he finally stood, pressing the creases out of his shorts with the palms of his hands, Stein stood too. He held out the figurine. That same almost-smile flickered across his face.

'Look after him for me, won't you. And do drop by again. To see me, I mean. I don't have many visitors here. This has been a treat. A rare treat.'

The van was parked crookedly at the kerb, and as Greg heaved himself up into the seat he tucked the figurine into the cubby on the dash. He could still see the top of its head, but at least it wasn't staring at him. The van started with a growl.

*

Janice listened intently as he told her about the encounter with Stein. Behind her he could see the waves hustling in to shore, the weeds bobbing in the swell. She'd told him that the movement calmed her thoughts, a natural sedative. When he mentioned the room full of figurines a shallow smile crept into her eyes, but he could tell that her mind was already visiting darker places. Once he'd finished she sat forward on the bench. Her eyes roamed his face as she twirled the pencil in her hair.

'And you're going to drop by his place again, right? You've looked in on him?'

'Briefly, yesterday. He seemed okay. You know, considering. He invited me in for coffee again, but they had me on a packed route that day. A couple of the guys are away. I had to cover ten extra blocks, you know how it is.'

'How did he seem?'

Greg didn't know. He'd knocked on Stein's door and hung around for an answer, the fear rising that he might be knocking for a dead man. But then the door opened. Stein had lost the tie. Otherwise little had changed. He found it so hard to read his facial expressions that he began to wonder whether he might have had cosmetic surgery.

'I don't think so. I mean, the guy's kinda hard to work out. Even you would struggle.'

'But he spoke to you? That's something, I guess.'

Janice was winding the pencil further and further into her hair, until it seemed inevitable that something must break. Greg laid his hand on hers and gently eased it down to her side. When he stood to leave she looked up.

'Just promise me you'll keep an eye on him? We're all more fragile than you think.'

Behind him he heard the hollow rattle of the sea sucking at the shore. He nodded, uncertain whether she could see or not.

*

Greg made 3788 Ostler part of his regular route over the following weeks, even when he didn't have a package to deliver. It seemed easier than having to lie to Janice every time she asked. Sometimes Stein answered, sometimes not. He didn't know where he went or what he did, but each time he'd sniff the air on his way back to the van, just in case.

It was on his tenth visit that Stein asked about the figurine. Greg didn't know what to say. He'd left the small porcelain gentleman in the cubby, and after a few days it had vanished. He couldn't believe that someone would have taken it.

'I have him at home. Really brightens up the room, you know? So thank you again. You didn't have to.'

Stein stretched his features into a smile. His eyes remained glassy.

'That's excellent to hear. Now do you have time for coffee? I have three new additions to the collection, if you'd like to see. One of them a rare Hummel.'

Greg paused. An image of Janice's disapproval flashed into his head.

'Sure. Only quickly though. They've got me running extra routes again today.'

The coffee was bitter but strong, its caffeinated fumes swirling around his head. Behind his right eyeball something ticked, as if someone kept flicking a switch. Stein had arranged three miniature porcelain statues along the tabletop. He was explaining their unique properties and potential value, but Greg couldn't concentrate. He wasn't Janice. He didn't have his sister's compulsion to nurture and heal. What was he doing here week after week? He sucked three deep breaths in through his nose, kneading the back of his neck with his fingers. The muscles felt tight.

'Listen, I have to go. These routes... They're keeping me busy. Thanks for the coffee. You need anything?'

'No, no, I'll do fine. Never been better. Just call by again.

Any time. And you'll take good care of that figurine I gave you?'

Greg felt the ticking behind his eye quicken. He was certain that Stein must be able to see it. After five steps down the path he knew it would seem strange to suddenly turn; after ten, it was impossible. When he got to the van he jumped into the cab and turned the key without looking back.

At the corner of the street he stopped, and screwed his thumb into his eye socket until the twitching subsided. Then he cracked his fist against the dashboard until the knuckles were red.

*

One morning when Greg unlocked his van the figurine was there again. Not tucked into the cubby, but standing on the dash, a smirk boasting of its uncanny disappearing act. Greg figured that someone had taken it home, but they had finally given up on it too. There wasn't much to love in its stiff limbs. Fat Brad must have replaced it when he collected the manifests.

It spent the morning on the dash, then he stashed in under his seat. Even then its ghost remained in the vacated spot, drawing Greg's eyes towards the nothingness where it had been.

When he got home the answering machine was blinking three messages. All from his sister.

*

Janice's house looked grey and washed-out in the fading light. He parked the van in a tight spot at the end of the row, then he spent a few minutes amending and signing off the day's paperwork. When he ran out of excuses he walked up to her porch and knocked on the screen door.

From inside he heard a scratching, then a hissing, then his sister's voice barking instructions. He waited until the inner door finally opened. Janice was bundled in several layers of woollens, the sleeves failing to hide three lines of fresh scratches along her forearms.

'Sorry, two new cats. I'm breaking them in, but I don't think they know it. One of them got feral with my slippers last night. You want to come in?'

Greg shook his head.

'I got your calls. Figured I should drop by. The routes they've got me running take me down Admiral anyways.'

'And? Have you checked in on our friend Mr Stein? How's he doing?'

He didn't know what to say. He'd spent the day composing lies and half-truths between stops on his route, turning the radio down to play out imaginary conversations in his head. The imaginary Janice was never happy with any of his answers. He didn't believe the real one would be either. The truth was that he couldn't face it any longer. He'd asked Fat Brad for a different route and he'd been given it without question. These days he didn't pass within a mile of 3788 Ostler. He avoided talking to the other drivers, or looking at the manifests for his old route. He even avoided the obituaries in the local newspaper.

'Don't be mad. I haven't seen him. They moved me from the route, and I can't spend all my spare hours holding the guy's hand. I have my life too.'

He could see the disappointment in her face, the way she withdrew her hands into the sleeves of her sweater. He could always read his sister's moods better than anyone. She wasn't thinking of his discomfort, the sleepless nights Stein had caused him. She just saw the dead guy slumped in the driver's seat. And her brother, the hero.

'I thought you might want this. It's really not my thing. I guess he'd want it to have a real home anyway, it doesn't look right at my place.'

Janice opened the door a crack and he passed the figurine through. Behind her one of the cats startled at the sound of the door creaking. She clutched the porcelain gentleman to her chest like a trophy.

'Sorry again, Jan. I can't keep pulling him out of that car. I just can't. Let me know if you need anything for the cats. And sorry.'

Greg turned and walked back down the porch steps, the shame burning through his collar. Beneath his feet the storm-weathered wood creaked and warped, and from the sea came a salty breeze, blowing away the smell of burnt gasoline.

TRAP

JUDY BIRKBECK

A fresh start. That the field gates had to be opened and shut every time didn't put me off, far from it. Paula struggled to heave the fourth and last gate with its broken hinge into a horizontal position and open it while I sat in the car and sheep with black faces and stockings and new-washed fluffy coats stared. Finally we stood outside the white cottage, a converted barn at the top of a two-mile dirt track, and looked over the treeless hills and snaking valleys of Upper Weardale. It was April and cold in the lungs. Burnhope Seat was capped with snow. Perfect for cross-country skiing in winter, I told her, the upper room with the skylight made the ideal studio and her artwork would be inspired by the views, I assured her when she looked dubious. She could paint the larches with their bright pink knobby female flowers. A pheasant squawked from the forest opposite. There were lambs in the valley and the nearest neighbours, at the farm, were a mile down the track. Then a curlew flew over with its melancholy call, scoops of pure sound that turned into a bubbling melody arcing over the dale. That decided me. Already a new musical composition was forming in my head.

I bought Paula a Dobermann for her protection when I was away. Jeeves was police-trained, but failed the tests. In my absence he pinned her to the bed every night with his sprawling six-stone body. More of a keeper than a guard dog.

Next time it was sunny we drove over to Cauldron Snout to see the thousands of spring gentians, little star-shaped royal-blue flowers among the withered, windswept grasses. They outshone the sky in blueness. It was the first time I had seen Paula excited since we'd moved in. She took out her sketch pad and I left her in her own little world and walked off on my own, humming a new melody and scribbling possible harmonies in my notebook. Back home, a smile lit up her face when she finished the watercolour. At dusk, out walking Jeeves in the forest, I saw a woodcock roding over the trees. Round and round it flew, making its sharp whistling and soft bass croaking sounds like a flute and a bassoon talking to each other. I knew it then. This place was a gift to an artist and a composer.

One day while she was out with Jeeves and her sketchpad, I went into her studio and looked through the stacked paintings till I came to the one hidden at the back, an oil painting: he had shoulder-length hair and a black shirt open at the neck, and a Byronic face with a nose that seemed to point up like a green woodpecker's beak. She didn't know I knew she still had this painting. I stared at it for a long time, till I heard the front door.

We became friends with the couple down the track, who owned most of the land. At first Pete was curmudgeonly. He looked like a skeleton with hollows round the backs of his eyes from using organophosphate sheep dips in the days when they were compulsory. But after I asked if he could fix our old heap of a generator, he was friendly. It was a relief to know Paula could always call on him in my frequent absences. We invited Pete and Bridget to dinner, leaving their older child to mind the two younger ones, and soon we established

Monopoly nights at their place with dinner and homemade parsnip wine. We brought the dinner on alternate occasions. Pete was local, but Bridget grew up five miles away and was considered an incomer, so God knows what people thought about us. Bridget was a homely sort, one of those fresh-faced women with butterbean-coloured hair and extra chins and ruby cheeks that, on closer inspection, are all broken capillaries, and I liked to think Paula could always drop in for a coffee. Bridget's fresh face was matched by a row of herbs and house plants in blooming health. 'Everything on this windowsill is happy,' she declared as she watered each one with precision. I hoped she and Paula would go shopping together, or whatever it is women do. We moaned to ourselves about the gates, but we never mentioned them to Pete and Bridget because they worked hard on the farm, while we appeared to loll about making art and music. The first time we went there for Monopoly, the little ones had been allowed to stay up to meet us. On the mantelpiece was a Mothering Sunday card from the five-year-old that read: 'I love you becos you do all hard werk.' Paula and I had chosen not to breed, as she already had grown-up children from a previous marriage. Pete always won at Monopoly. He never let anyone off their debts. 'Winner takes all,' he said with a grin as he counted his stack of £500 notes.

Returning from the San Francisco performance of a short orchestral piece, its US première, I found Paula working on a new watercolour of a pheasant with gleaming copper plumage. She called him Philip. He'd discovered the food dropped by siskins and tits on the fat block, so she put down extra for him every morning. With the applause still ringing in my ears, I took Jeeves for a walk the mile and a half to the mailbox down the track which followed the Killhope Burn. The burn spoke to me. The clean, fresh air after city grime and the sight of Paula contented put me in a creative mood. The stream babbled and the snowy-chested dippers bobbed on the tumbling boulders and plunged in after caddis-fly larvae or zipped upstream with piercing squeaks like a piccolo.

Back at the cottage, the new piece in my head led me straight to the piano with the music manuscript pad, and when Paula came in I raised a hand to silence her. I'd make it up to her later.

He was still there, at the back of the stack with his noble features, the hair flopping over his high forehead. She had taken the gentians and other pictures in the search for a local gallery, but not him. She came back radiant. A gallery in Ireshopeburn loved the gentians and wanted more local landscapes. We drove up to the high moor and a hen harrier glided low above our heads, making strafing sounds, so low I could clearly see its owl-like face. Perhaps we were near a nest. We moved further off to watch it planing and swooping, and basked in the sun like adders. I was writing the second slow movement of a new sonata and its graceful flight inspired me.

'You look different,' Bridget told me one Monopoly night. Paula stared. My hand went to my throat, where I had unbuttoned the new black shirt. 'Maybe it's your hair. It's grown.'

'Time for a haircut,' said Paula.

'I think I might let it grow.'

Pete took all the property as usual. It was Bridget's fault, letting him off debts, letting him pay later.

'Winner takes all,' he said and grinned.

'And you always do, Pete,' I said.

Those hazy days did not last. Walking together in the forest one time, we heard muted squeals coming from the bracken and found a weasel caught in a gin trap. Its leg was almost severed, the white bone bared. Its eyes were half-closed, fur streaked with sweat, jaws slightly open. There was blood round its mouth where it had tried to bite the trap. An ear flapped. Sometimes it struggled. Paula moved to release it, but

I held her back. It wouldn't survive. We stood helplessly while it made feeble efforts to move. It was unbearable. Paula took a photo on her phone.

'Come on,' I said and dragged her away. 'Nature is raw in tooth and claw.'

'That's not nature,' she replied. 'Those leg-hold traps have been illegal for decades.'

She went every day to photograph the weasel. Reluctantly I went with her. She grew more upset each time. They were supposed to check traps daily, not that there was anyone but us to see. It was two days before it died, but a week before the body was removed. Paula was heartbroken. She painted the long body lying limply on a bed of larch and pine needles, its white belly exposed, the bloody leg in the foreground, each vicious tooth of the gin trap painted black. The gallery rejected it.

She informed the police, but they needed evidence of who set the trap.

'I have photos with dates showing that no one checked for seven days,' she screamed. 'I have photos of an illegal gin trap.'

'Let's go,' I said, gripping her arm so tightly the skin bunched up.

Pete sympathised. The gamekeeper was notorious.

We avoided the forest, walked down the steep gills along by the hope-burns, over to the falls to see the sea-trout jumping up, or drove to Whitfield Moor where there were golden plovers. They made no tune, but their sad piping calls echoed across the sky. We picked bilberries and Paula drew empty moorland.

Philip lay dead on the path with a bullet in his belly. I was away when it happened. Thankfully Pete and Bridget were there for coffee and comfort, but Paula was inconsolable. I said it's only a pheasant, that's the way most of them go, but she said the gamekeeper had done it out of spite. It came out that she still walked in the forest, without Jeeves for fear of his getting injured, and had found another gin trap which she triggered shut with a stick, and snares which she cut with wire-cutters. One snare was round a skeleton with fur attached, which couldn't have been checked for weeks. She'd seen the gamekeeper from a distance. She had no proof he'd shot Philip, just felt it in her bones, by the scowl on the retreating figure's face. Paula's obsession with the traps and Philip punctured my elation at the success of the UK première in Manchester of what I called The Dipper Sonata. Her upset was out of proportion to the death of a pheasant. There must be something else going on here. I pushed my forelock out of my eyes and tried to reason with her. Travelling is exhausting and I wasn't expecting this trouble, so Monopoly should have been a relief, but the atmosphere was tainted. Maybe it was the wine talking. There was the usual banter about Pete's business acumen, till Bridget drew a card saying she'd won second prize in a beauty contest. She mock-preened herself.

Pete spluttered. 'I hate to think what the rest were like,' he said.

Paula and I tittered, not taking it seriously, and I made dissenting noises, although Bridget's hair smelt like Dettol and looked like a moorland tree, short and squat with a wedge at the back. The wind sculpted everything here.

Bridget said, 'You should go to jail, not pass go and not collect £200, because that's where traitors go.'

We all laughed, but the game went downhill after. I felt as though we'd stumbled into a domestic. By contrast, Paula and I seemed close and I was eager to get to bed, so we left early, but in bed Paula made excuses and turned away. I lay awake, every cell in my body on fire and my cock raring to go. Unable to sleep, I got up and looked out at the light of a distant farmstead. The moon was ashen with a rainbow halo. To anyone else the empty landscape would have looked lonely, but I loved it here. Our old life was a tornado of dinner parties, shopping for Armani suits and Louis Vuitton handbags, and showing off at the opera. You couldn't know who you were in all that turbulence. It was boring and my audiences disappointed me. Up here I could wander, rugged as the land, and new compositions came tumbling into my head.

The generator thumped away, every so often misfiring. In Paula's studio a new picture stood on the easel: a squirrel caught in a snare. The wire loop had sunk so deep it was invisible. In its place was a bloody necklace. The back legs stretched out behind. She'd painted it in oils, so life-like I could almost reach out and touch the sweaty fur. I looked through the stack against the wall. More trapped animals, and him. I pushed my hair behind my ears and went outside. In the night sky, clouds scooped themselves into shapes like jellyfish holding hands with wispy fingers.

On my return from a performance of The Golden Plover Sonata in Manchester, I got out to open each gate, drove through and shut it. I was looking forward to telling Paula about the standing ovation I'd received when I went up on stage. The sun lit up the snow on Burnhope Seat. How lucky I was to live in this beautiful place, with a beautiful wife to look after it for me. I parked the Rover. The generator still chugged and sputtered, on its last legs. Jeeves was not there to welcome me, nor Paula, so I guessed they were out for a walk. Outside, I stood swaying on the grass, but I couldn't spot them coming up the track. A curlew flew over, with its trilling melody arcing over the uplands. It was leaving, heading for the coast for the winter.

I went back in and up to the studio. It was flooded with light but empty – no easel, no paints. All that remained was pictures of trapped animals. The lover at the back of the stack had gone. On the table was a note: 'Sorry, I'm in love with Pete. Bridget will fill you in.' My good humour evaporated like the fish dissipating in the burn when I approached. I had been like a bubble floating along, not thinking about the final pop.

And after all I had done for Paula. I wandered down along Killhope Burn where the dippers still bobbed and walked into the water, but heard no music. I should have left her after the first time.

SCAPEGOAT

TIM LOVE

Once again I wake, want to go home, realise I am home, have a shower to wash away the tears. Like the bell of a goat who can't distinguish the ringing from his walking, my Self tinkles through my waking hours. Even at night the wind sometimes catches it as I dream.

I don't know what I'd do without work to distract me. Today as usual I've spent the morning hammering the keyboard for all it's worth. At the coffee break our team meets in the office kitchen. The first to arrive has boiled the kettle and turned the TV onto a news channel in case conversation flags. I say nothing until it's worth saying. I'm not embarrassed by silence. I don't like those who'd rather spout tripe than listen. Mark in particular talks drivel. It's a crisis day for the Euro. Italy's in trouble. I mention that if they sold Berlusconi-shaped pasta their GDP problem would disappear overnight. A good enough joke, I think. The others describe novelty pasta shapes that they'd seen on holiday, mostly naughty ones from Pisa and Pompeii. Al dente, ha ha. I say that it's a pity that our investment products weren't naughtier.

Silence. Our company is in trouble. Perhaps my workmates are wondering if their own job's at risk. 'Time to hump more shares,' says Mark, swilling his Star Wars cup and slamming it on the draining board. People drift off, leaving me alone with Lucy, our newest recruit. I've been making more jokes since she's arrived. Perhaps I'm trying to impress her. She's filling the sink with hot water. There are rumours on the grapevine that she's available. I have been stealing glances at her to check if she's really as beautiful as she looks. When she smiles, her jawbone's too straight compared to the curve of her lips. I noticed during the chit-chat that she sometimes breathed in exaggeratedly - a sign that she wanted to speak. The others didn't notice. Now she has her chance.

'Is Mark married?' she asks, while we rattle the cups into the sink. I squirt some Fairy Liquid in. Because she's recently arrived, her job might be the most secure. Or maybe she'll be the first to get sacked.

'I don't know,' I say, 'but I've played squash with him and he's hung like a horse.'

'Pity his monthly revenue isn't as impressive,' she says as she turns away.

Our job is to make money. Big money. We lose it too. Sometimes I recover it later than the records show. The company understands the advantages in granting us this freedom. Our little team makes more money in a year than the whole of Stoke does. We are why the government daren't overtax the rich. We work in cubicles, slurp Nescafé at break-time, and burn out by 35, our best years gone. I don't have long left.

During the afternoon I wonder how the break has affected my relationship with Lucy. On the plus side she stayed behind after the others left. On the other hand she's treating me like a sexless confidant, a snitch. If only she knew that I'm a different person at work to who I am at home.

I've learnt which traffic lights let me through the quickest; that if I sneak off 5 minutes early I miss the rush. I make the most of it.

*

A girl's restocking the Christmas Pudding shelves when a man approaches.

'Excuse me. I want to see the manager.'

'Sorry sir, I think he's busy right now.'

'Hello,' interrupts a man in a suit. 'I'm Gordon Spense, the acting manager today and I happened to be passing. How can I help?'

'It's that music.'

The girl walks away.

'I didn't catch your name sir.'

'Jack Hayward. It's about that ruddy music.'

'I'm sure you appreciate that all supermarkets play festive songs at this time of year.'

'It's the one that goes *Next year all your troubles will be out of sight.*'

'Well yes, we want people to look forward to better times.'

'I've got troubles Gordon, big troubles. Six months to live. Next Christmas all my troubles will be long gone.'

'I'm very sorry to hear that Mr Hayward.'

'Are you married Gordon?'

The manager shakes his head.

'I was. 12 years. That's 12 Merry Little Christmases, Gordon. Just one more to go.'

'It must be distressing for you. I'll see what I can do about that song, Mr Hayward,' says the manager, lifting a hamper from a nearby display. 'Please, take this with our compliments. I understand how it is. Sounds like you need a holiday.'

'Thankyou, Gordon, you're a decent fellow,' the man says, struggling out with the hamper. The manager turns away, walks along the aisles, approaches the girl who'd been restocking, looks at her breasts, her name-badge.

'You're new here Susan, aren't you?'

*

Details congregate at extremities - the footnotes of a page; the end of a story; down the arm to fingerprints; along a motorway to a B road then my cottage where smells aren't suppressed. They rise to greet me as I enter each room - thatch, French Polish, yesterday's left-over curry. I like it here. The other me takes over, the one who cherishes old things, who prepares jokes and lists, who draws diagrams with arrows showing how perfectly the Self corresponds to a phantom limb, both causing pain.

Some people love supermarkets - getting everything from one place even if it's not all very good. It's like being married I suppose. But I shop around. My favourite street leads out of town, when the barbers, betting shops and second-hand vinyl stores take over, where people queue for Poundland clearance sales. It's different each time I go: a bingo hall becomes a Mosque, a junkshop has just one book in the window, entitled 'Growing your own moustache', a pub advertizes a Thursday night of Faggots and Peas. Leading up to Christmas the shops hang on, the way old people hang on. I know a little cheese shop there. The owners visit their daughter back in France once a month, returning with a vanload of Bries, Camemberts, Saint Paulin and Minolettes bought straight from little farms. My favourite days are when I arrive while they're still unwrapping. Some cheeses travel better than others. They offer me slivers, asking for a second opinion. I'm amazed their business survives. I've hardly seen a customer there. It's a labour of love. I admire that. The French are so much more refined than Italians – for a start they don't have Gorgonzola ice-cream.

I empty the hamper, checking the cheese first. Plain cheddar. Yuck. The phone rings. A man asks me if I'm Mr

Hayward. I say 'No. Are you?' No, he says, laughing, he's John, and he can help me. He asks if I've ever considered Solar Panels. I say 'Do you bastards ever think what you might be interrupting when you phone? After a day's work do you go home happy with your contributions to society? You're scum. When my father had cancer he rushed to the phone when it rang, thinking it might be me, his only surviving relative, but when he picked it up it was a bag of shit like you. Maybe it *was* you. Why don't you find a job that leaves you with a shred of self respect. Do you have someone who cares about you? No, of course you don't. If you did, you wouldn't act like a thoughtless fucking wanker. What are you going to do after this call? Phone the next person on the list I bet, another person dying of cancer. Do me a favour and don't leave them in tears this time. Have you had cancer John? Just you wait. Have you watched someone you love suffer? No, because you're incapable of love. You're making me suffer, and that's not good. Change your life John. Fuck off.'

*

I'm first to the kitchen today. Lucy soon arrives, as if she's been waiting for me. Despite the weather she's in short sleeves. Even her arms are beautiful. Each time she turns away I trace the contours from her surprisingly muscular shoulders slowly down to her delicate fingers. No ring. Someone should make a sculpture of her arms and display them in the Louvre next to the Venus de Milo.

'I couldn't help noticing,' she says, 'that in the files your name is 'Sil Ozla'. Turkish?'

'No, though my father was German.'

'Aren't they playing England tonight?'

'Yes, but my name's not German. You see, when I was young I wanted a personalised number plate. I discovered it was much cheaper to change my name than change car. Now that I'm rich enough to buy any car I like – a fleet of them in fact – I might change my mind again.'

The others drift in.

'Are your parents still alive?' Lucy asked.

'No. Actually, I'm still emptying my father's place out. It's a gold-mine. Tidying his loft I found an old photo of him with a woman who looked familiar. On the back was 'July 16th, 1950', when my father was still in Canada. He'd emigrated there from Germany before in the war. He kept diaries in those days so I looked up that entry and found he'd talked to Vera Lynn.'

'Lucky man,' says Mark, 'Our gallant lads all admired her. She did lots of charity work you know.'

'But the weird thing was the conversation they had. My father wrote it all down. She asked him where he came from originally with that accent. He said Leipzig and she asked which part. He said 'Off the Kornstrasse,' and she replied 'Not Konigborn by any chance'. That was where my father was born. She knew more about Germany than people realise. She recorded fourteen songs in German you know. When I went to Germany in September to see where my father was brought up, I tried a few houses on the street in case anyone knew our family. At number 87 a young couple had only recently moved in. They said that the previous owner, Lotte Hacke, had lived there for over eighty years. They'd not cleared out the loft and invited me to go up there. So I kitted myself out and searched. Inside a mildewed suitcase were some letters in English. I recognised the handwriting from the papers I'd been researching - Vera Lynn's. The two of them were pen friends. The local authorities in Leipzig were very helpful. Some of Hacke's papers were in their museum. You see, Hacke had been an informer. She'd informed on my father, which is why he left. When I returned to England I contacted the Imperial War Museum's Vera Lynn collection. Amongst Lynn's interests were painting, swimming and gardening. Hacke sent her seeds - rare alpine flowers. The really interesting thing was what Hacke wrote for the Gestapo - reports on English army camps during the summer of 1942: June - Colchester and Newmarket; July - Barnstable and Leeds, which corresponded exactly with Lynn's visits.'

'Amazing. But why would Vera do that?' asks Mark.

'Perhaps she saw the continuation of the war as the only way to prolong her fame, or perhaps she didn't realise she was passing on anything useful.'

'Maybe the government was telling her what to say,' says Lucy, 'So what will you do next?'

'Well, I don't want to go public until I'm sure.'

'If you're wrong,' says Mark, 'you'll get thrown off the White Cliffs of Dover.'

'If I'm wrong, I'll throw myself off. Anyway back to work.'

During the afternoon it amuses me to think that Mark believed the story. Its length must have convinced him. I worry however about how Lucy will take it when she finds out I've juped her too. Of course I was joking about throwing myself off. I know the public hate people like me - I read about it in the papers. But if I didn't earn those bonuses their investments wouldn't earn much interest. They couldn't live without me. I'm performing a public service at great personal sacrifice. I love it.

*

He'd discovered where Lucy lives, and that the central library has a café on the top floor whose windows overlook her flats. He'd watched the woman behind the counter, learnt her routines. Tonight he buys a tea there. At closing time he says goodbye to her as he returns his cup, but stays just outside the café door. He slips back in as she busies herself in the kitchen area, and hides in a blind-spot. He hears her drag a bin liner out and close the door. He waits for the noises to fade, then aims his binoculars at the flats. At 8.15 some lights come on.

He sees Lucy moving around the kitchen. Then she pulls the blinds down. A few minutes later the lights in the next room come on. She's watching a TV whose screen he can't see. He turns on his little radio, inserts an earphone. He can tell by her movements that she's watching the same game delayed by a few seconds. When it finishes she turns everything off and goes into the bedroom. Within 20 minutes all the lights are out.

He spends an uncomfortable night on the lino, sustained by the thought that she only watched the match to have an excuse to talk with him about it. He hadn't realised how many radio stations played all through the night. He sleeps fitfully, using just one earpiece so that he can also hear sounds in the building. Around midnight he hears barks, thinks that they're coming from inside the building, but they never come closer. He grows hungry. For breakfast he tries the sugar sachets and tiny milk containers that the café lady has left out. He looks across at the flat. Lucy's sitting in a bathrobe having toast and coffee. Someone comes in, drying their hair, hugging Lucy from behind. You'd expect it to be Mark. In fact, it's that girl from the supermarket.

As soon as the library opens he slips out of the café. If he's seen coming downstairs he'll just say that he popped up there for a coffee, not realising that it was shut until 10 on Saturdays. He's thought of everything - his mind is a flowchart full of arrows and possibilities. The relief of realising he'd taken a chance and got away with it makes him hungrier still. He drives to the cheese shop. Outside he pauses, notices a young woman behind the counter. She's wearing a sort of tennis dress with a scalloped neckline. She's doing a crossword or maybe a Sudoku, tapping her pen against the side of her nose. Her features are familiar. He goes in, starts chatting, asks if she's Jacques' daughter.

'Yes! My parents have popped to London, so I'm looking after the shop for a day or two. All on my owneo.'

'Busy?'

'What do you think.'

'Your parents never said what you do in France.'

'I'm a model. But they don't care about that. All that worries them is that I'm still not married.'

He thinks he's expected to express amazement at this. He's distracted not by her expressive arm gestures but how they make her breasts sway - she can't be wearing a bra.

'So why did they move here, your parents?'

'My mother taught French and my father became a rep for some French firms, but that wasn't their plan. I don't think they had a plan. They'd heard about the Beatles and wanted a new life.'

He asks for Crottin de Chavignol because it's at the front of the display cabinet between them. When she leans to unwrap the cheese her dress falls forward. He sees not only her breasts but beyond her flat stomach, her knickers. She's not wearing a ring. She's alone in the shop. She's French. He's a family friend. He miscalculates. He won't be shopping there again.

*

What so impresses me about Dover Castle is how it summarizes English history, how it survived by adapting. It was once an Iron Age hill fort. A cylindrical Roman lighthouse built to save sailors evolved into the spire of an Anglo-Saxon church built to save souls. William the Conqueror stockaded the site. Henry II built the main castle with a keep like you see in children's drawings or a dream. Tunnels were dug in medieval times. During the Napoleonic wars they were extended for miles. Operation Dynamo - the Rescue from Dunkirk - was coordinated from the warren of tunnels. In the event of nuclear war, it would have been a Regional Seat of Government - project Dumpy. The BBC had a TV studio there. Diluted by all that history I feel insignificant.

I go on all the tours. I especially enjoy the underground hospital and the home-made ice-cream in the café. I stand on the terrace. There's a beautifully clear sky. If it's possible to see France, today's the day. I'm not sure, not yet. I take from my pocket the official envelope that Lucy, with all the regret she could muster, gave me at tea-break, tear it into little pieces and let one fall over the railings to test the wind direction. Still. Almost perfect. A distant church bell clangs. No, it's coming from below. Looking down the cliff-face I can just make out a goat, white against white, perched on a ledge. God knows how it got there. There must be a secret path. It looks up at me imploringly, opens its mouth as if asking for help but then stretches to pluck the piece of paper from the air. It must be hungry. I drop another piece, reaching over as far as I can to see if the goat will cope. Then further.

YOU MAY AS WELL GIVE UP TRYING TO MAKE SOMETHING OF YOURSELF

GORDON COLLINS

'Listen, darling. I've got some bad news,' I said to my wife in the kitchen when I returned from the hospital.

'Right,' Rachel said but she didn't stop what she was doing. She was scooping the jam out of a jar with a spoon and putting it into Tupperware. She buys this really nice jam in a nice jar and then she empties it into Tupperware, not even a jar. When I asked her about it she said that she didn't want her jam in a jar.

'They said it was best to have it taken out,' I said.

'Have what taken out?'

'My kidney.'

'Right,' she said. The spoon made a 'schloop' sound as she scooped out the dark red jam.

'Probably next week,' I said.

'I need the car next week.'

'It's OK. I can get the bus. They said it was routine and it shouldn't take long.'

'Right.'

She has her own way of dealing with bad news. I thought

about cuddling her but I didn't. 'I'm sure it will all be alright,' I said.

'OK. OK. Kidney out next week.'

She washed the spoon, clicked the lid on the Tupperware and threw the jar in the recycling bin without washing it out properly. Then she opened another jar.

'Do you want me to do that?' I asked.

She stopped and she looked at me and did that thing where she pushed her cheek out with her tongue. 'No. Of course I don't,' she said.

'Sorry,' I said and I went upstairs to my room.

*

She did come and visit me after the operation though. I was still drowsy from the anaesthetic and so I can't quite remember but the nurses said she had been. The operation had gone well. The doctor said that I shouldn't have any more problems and that I would be fine with only one kidney if I looked after myself. He gave me some antibiotics and patted me on the hand and smiled. I don't like not sleeping in my own bed and so I was happy when he said I could be discharged that day. They still had to do lots of tests on blood pressure and stuff but I suppose they have to be safe. Eventually they let me go. I got dressed but I couldn't find any of my stuff. I'd left my wallet, keys and phone in the cupboard-on-wheels by my bed but they were all gone. None of the nurses knew anything about it. They rang home but there was no answer. I had to wait for ages because they had to have a meeting about it. After that, they said I should cancel my cards and then they gave me a form and said not to worry about it today but to go home and sort it all out tomorrow. Rachel still wasn't answering the phone and so I had to borrow money for the bus home from a special fund they have at the hospital. Then it was a ten-minute walk from the bus stop and my side hurt every step because the doctors had said I shouldn't really walk very far and I could see why.

Rachel answered the door. 'Oh it's you,' she said as if she wasn't expecting me and she pushed me away.

'Careful, please!' I said, noticing my wallet and phone on the table by the door.

'What do you want?' she asked.

'What do you mean? I live here.'

'No. No. No. The hospital was meant to deal with this. Oh. OK. Come in,' she said and she let me in and sat me on the sofa. 'Just stay there while I figure out what to do with you.' She went upstairs to the bedroom and was talking to someone. I tried to listen but I was so tired that I dozed off.

When I woke up she was standing there, wearing her tall boots and holding a kidney in her hands.

'Right you, Richard and I don't think you should be here,' she said.

'What?' My name is Richard and I hadn't decided this, obviously. 'What do you mean?'

'You're. Well, you're extraneous,' she said.

'No I'm not.'

'You are. So have a rest and then I think it's best if you leave, OK?'

'Is that my kidney?'

She looked at me weirdly. Then I noticed that the kidney had my watch around it. 'Hey! It's wearing my watch'.

'No. It's Richard's watch.'

'But I'm Richard.'

'No. This is Richard. You are Richard's arms, head, liver etc.'

'What? No. I'm Richard. That's my kidney which I had extracted.'

'Richard doesn't see it that way. He considers that he had you extracted.'

The kidney just sat in her hand wearing my watch.

'That's ridiculous.'

'Is it?'

'Yes. Of course it is?'

'Why?'

'I have the brain and all the bits that move. Just by volume, I'm clearly the greater part so I had him extracted and not vice versa.'

'Look. We could argue all day about who extracted who and who's got more cognitive skills. At the end of the day it's up to me which one of you I consider to be my husband and, let's face it, I didn't marry you for your intellect or your motility. Now, what's the time?'

I looked at my wrist but there was no watch on it because my kidney was wearing it.

'Oh!' Rachel laughed as she realised this. 'We'd better go or we'll be late for the restaurant. Richard is taking me to La Gourade. So if you could just lock up when you leave.'

La Gourade! We were going to go there for our anniversary but it was too expensive. 'No. I'm not going. This is my house and I'm –'

She held her finger to her mouth and shushed me. 'You're being a little scary. I think you should just go. It's weird talking to body parts. Really the hospital should have disposed of you,' she said.

'You can't make me!' I shouted and I ran upstairs and locked myself in my room. I heard the front door close and I went to the window to see the car go off. *She* was driving.

*

I was still in my room when they returned. I could hear them laughing and giggling. She was drunk and making flirty little squeaky noises. I wanted to see what they were doing but I didn't dare leave my room and so I put on my headphones and listened to my 90s indie playlist which she doesn't like and I just wore underwear and my robot T-shirt which she also doesn't like. I kept turning the music down to listen to them and turning it back up again because every time I did this they were making louder and ruder noises. I felt awful even though she wasn't technically being unfaithful to me, I supposed.

In the morning I woke up when I heard the front door again. I looked out of the window and saw her driving off to work. I went downstairs – I made sure I didn't look in the bedroom. I put some bread in the toaster and turned on the radio – they were talking about expulsions in schools. I thought about what to cook for dinner. The best thing to do would be to just carry on as normal and then hope everything would calm down this evening.

Rachel had put the kidney on the sofa and switched on the TV for it. I chopped onions and carrots in the kitchen. I was making shepherds' pie which was Rachel's favourite. The kidney was just watching property programmes one after another. 'You'll never afford anything like that,' I thought. On one of the programs the couple really liked the fire place in a terraced house in a nice area but the house was too small for their requirements. The developers knocked it all down, apart from the fire place, and then built one of those 'open plan' houses around the fireplace. It did look nice. They could get cosy in front of the fire or just walk to the kitchen without opening any doors.

I watched that property program and then another one came on. I sat with my kidney next to me, only 20cm to the left of where it used to be when it was an internal organ. In the next programme, a couple were having an extension done except they changed their minds and they made the extension an annex which the man used as a studio. Except, when the film crew came back in a month's time, his wife had hung the washing up in the annex and the husband was inside watching television. The presenter made it seem funny, though.

There was a knock on the door which I thought would be my new cactus delivery but it was Melanie, Rachel's sister, who was the best person who could possibly come round at that moment. I like Melanie. We both love Rachel but we both understand her moods and so we can support each other.

'Is Richard in?'

'*I'm* Richard,' I said.

'Yeah, yeah. Sure. Can I come in?'

'Of course.' I let her in and made her tea in the kitchen.

'I heard that your operation didn't go well.'

'It was fine.'

'Really? I heard that they extracted you and not your kidney.'

'No. No. That's not right. But Rachel seems to think so. Oh, Mel, I don't know what's got into her.'

'Well. You know how she is. Is your kidney at home?'

'Yes. He's just there,' I said, pointing to the sofa.

'Great,' she said. She picked him up and went off into the bedroom. I followed her but she shut the door on me.

They were in there all afternoon while I cooked the shepherd's pie and I also did the laundry. The washing machine is quite loud and so I couldn't hear everything in the bedroom. Mel came out after an hour, quickly said goodbye to me and left. I had a cup of tea and watched another property program on my own.

Rachel came back at five twenty as usual. 'Where is he?' she asked.

'In the bedroom,' I told her.

She went straight to the main bedroom and screamed. 'What did you do to him?' Rachel shouted at me.

I rushed through to the bedroom. The kidney lay on the floor. A pair of my underwear lay loosely around it and a spot of blood stained the waistband.

'What did you do to him?' Rachel shouted at me again.

'It was Mel. She came round earlier,' I said.

Rachel kneeled down next to the kidney and cradled it in her hands and brought it to her cheek. She stayed like that for a while. She wasn't crying, though. She was examining it, squeezing it and bending it.

'I'm sorry,' I said and went back to the kitchen.

After that, Rachel gave up work. She said that she couldn't cope with going in. Most days she didn't even get dressed. I tried to cheer her up. I suggested we go to La Gourade but that made her cry. I said we could move to a bigger house nearer to the park. I even put our house on the market, even though we couldn't really afford anything better. I bought her ice cream and flowers but she barely said thank you.

Every morning I would feel her touching my side but she would stop as soon as she knew I was awake. She'd stop and sigh and slump back onto her side and sometimes lay there all morning. Sometimes I pretended to still be asleep.

'She'll get there,' Mel said when I met her for coffee in one of the cafés near her work in town. 'She's just got to go through this in her own way. The worst thing you can do is to force her.'

'Do you really think she'll come back to me?'

'Yes. There's something in you. You really can't see it can you? You've got something so special inside you,' she said and she hugged me which she didn't usually do, and so that felt especially reassuring. As she stopped hugging me her hand rested on the left side of my lower back and she squeezed it a little which I found a bit odd.

I told Rachel about it when I got back. She didn't say anything and so I went to my room and started to re-pot some small Aloes. After a while, Rachel knocked and then came in.

'Richard?'

'Yes?' I said. She hadn't called me Richard since it happened.

'I don't want you to see Mel anymore.'

'What? Why not?'

'Please. Please don't see Mel anymore,' she said.

'Ok. If that's what you want.'

'Thank you,' she said and she hugged me. 'You're *my* man,' she said.

MY KNEE

JOHN D RUTTER

My knee hurts quite badly. It's all flooding back now the way the pain starts when you stub your toe, you know it's coming but there's a pause before it bites.

Pippa and I had been out for dinner at the French. We'd been civilised all evening, given the circumstances, and had managed to eat without arguing, without phones. Good wine always helps. I still had my grey suit on and she wore a tight-fitting black skirt. She's been dressing smarter for work this year, always wears lipstick. We kept the conversation to siblings and work.

We didn't talk about the situation at all.

An evening of calm before the impending crisis, that's what we'd agreed. I'd done a good job of keeping things sensible for the last month while she sorted herself out. But something was bound to happen with Pippa around.

We were almost back at the house (my house I suppose I should start calling it). I'd won the argument that she'd drive. It was only fair I had a drink and she was still feeling guilty. Besides I didn't like being in my car with her after that time she borrowed it one Sunday, 'to meet some German visitors at the airport,' with her boss. His Merc. only has two seats, her Mini was too small.

Then, as we arrived at the hump-backed bridge at the end of our street – my street soon – it happened. This is where Pippa announced, 'I could live round here!' when we first came to look at houses in Hale three years ago.

A car came *flying* over the bridge, none of the wheels were touching the floor! I felt a surge of adrenalin. It was like someone had their finger on freeze frame. Like the night I first found out.

Pippa let go of the steering wheel, covered her face and screamed. The other car squealed and hit us with a thump. It made a vicious noise; screeching, smashing, crunching; an oddly exhilarating moment. Then a prolonged hiss and the news still playing on the car radio.

A woman was stabbed repeatedly...

Was she alright? The seatbelt had tugged at my chest but I was fine. I could see Pippa wasn't hurt but she was hysterical. 'My Mini!' she said. 'She's killed my Mini!' The windscreen had been smashed to an opaque mosaic.

... pronounced dead at the scene.

The other driver, another young woman, was already out of her car and was staring at the wreckage.

... officer said, 'This was a sustained and frenzied attack...'

I turned the radio off.

'Are you alright?' I asked Pippa. I put my hand on hers. She pulled it away and rummaged for her phone. The phone I bought her last Christmas. Look at the thanks I got.

'I'm alright, but look at the state of my car!'

I reached over, turned the ignition off and took the key out.

My car? Strictly speaking it should go down as a marital asset. The Audi is a company car so technically the Mini was *our* car. And I'd paid for it last year with my bonus back when business was good. My solicitor said it was best to list that kind of thing in case hers started getting funny about pensions and such. I told him I didn't want any conflict. It's always better to avoid that. It's always better to avoid that.

I unfastened the seat belt.

I hadn't even been angry at Pippa when I first found out. I'd nipped out for a quick pint at the Griffin and I saw the Mini snuggled up to his flashy Merc. Vince, her boss. (Personalised number plate!)

I swung the door open and got out of the car.

An Anne Summers party in Bury, she'd told me. Please show me a *bit* of respect. When she came clattering in about midnight I challenged her. She hadn't even bought anything. People always buy something, don't they? And what would she need that kind of thing for anyway? She had too much red lipstick on.

The wind slapped my face.

First thing she did when I confronted her with my clues was to laugh. She said it was a nervous laugh. I poured her the last of the wine and opened another bottle and we sat and talked at the kitchen table. She didn't say anything about me drinking for once. She confessed what she'd done in my car. She said she hoped I could find a way to forgive her. I said there's no point in getting angry.

There was a whiff of petrol and smoke in the air.

Before I could get round to the mangled front of the Mini the other woman had started shouting at Pippa through the window, pointing her blood-red fingernails and wagging her shaggy blonde hair. What was she shouting about? It wasn't Pippa's fault. The woman had on those black leggings that Pippa always wears – they didn't look as good on her.

I could smell burning rubber.

What the hell were you doing?' the woman shouted in a Manchester accent.

There's no need to shout like that.

Now Pippa was out and squaring up to her.

'You've smashed my bloody car in, you stupid cow!' When she was angry she lapsed into Essex instead of her usual how-now-brown-cow. It was the same when she cried. There'd been a lot of that recently. She kept asking what was going to happen to her. I've been more than fair about the house and the money after what she's done to me.

The other girl was grabbing her.

'Who are you calling a cow?'

I stepped between them before things got out of hand. I've had plenty of practice calming people down recently. Al, when he said, 'He can be like that,' perhaps he had a point. And Pippa's mum, Bunny, she got all teary too. I'm the one that loses half my family. I'll probably never see them again. If I can keep control why can't everyone else?

'Calm down,' I said. 'There's no need to get excited…'

'What it got to do with you?' Now the woman was rearing up at me. 'You stink of booze!'

You can only push me so far.

Pippa stepped forward again. 'What's that got to do with anything?'

'Has she been drinking too?'

'It's your fault, you were going too fast!' Pippa said.

'Look, let's all stay calm and get this sorted out,' I said. 'Is anyone hurt?'

The woman said, 'I'm not hurt, but look at the state of my car. You'll have to pay for it!'

Pippa started crying, bent over the Mini's gnarled wheel arch. I put my arm around her. She shrugged it off.

'It'll be alright,' I said. 'We'll get the insurance sorted and everything will be alright.'

'Yeh! I want your insurance,' The woman said.

'You were on the wrong side of the road,' I said, quietly but firmly.

'So were you!'

'No I wasn't,' Pippa cried. 'Look where the cars are!'

The Mini was kissing the kerb, its cute face ruined. The other car, a dirty black Golf, was slewn diagonally across the centre line, the front embedded in the Mini. Pippa's bumper had come off altogether, her blue bonnet was twisted out of shape. The headlights were smashed.

'That's where you swerved!'

I raised my arms to show everyone to simmer down. Even when Pippa got upset about furniture and having to find a new flat I was in control. Someone has to be rational.

'Let's swap insurance details and wait till the police get here,' I said.

'What do you want the police for?' The woman screamed. 'It's not my fault. It's that road!'

'Actually there have been a few accidents here.' I said. I wondered why she was being so aggressive, defensive really. It is a known accident spot, you can't see who's coming from the opposite direction.

Pippa was clutching her phone to her ear. Did she have to call? Now?

Some idiot beeped their horn. For Christ's sake!

By now there were cars stopped on both sides of the bridge. The man that lives three doors down, BMW driver, personal injury solicitor, was directing traffic and telling everyone what had happened.

'Is everyone alright? May I help, I'm a solicitor.'

Show off! It's like that at work, Andrew, the FD, he's another, pointing out people's mistakes.

'I don't think anyone's injured,' I said.

Show-off spoke to the other woman then he went over and put his greedy arm round Pippa's shoulder. Why's it always about her? She'd gone round there to sit with his girlfriend a couple of times over the last month. It's hard enough without involving anyone else. I hadn't even shouted at her. I was letting her have all the best crockery and glasses (I'd typed a list). I'd have preferred it if people just left us alone. First that smug pair sticking their noses in, now this.

It started spitting.

The woman was examining her car, it looked like she was going to start blubbing too, she was muttering under her breath.

It was after ten and I had to get ready for the Friday Fright (our weekly roasting) before I could go bed. The last couple of meetings hadn't gone very well. I've had a lot on my mind. Now I was going to have to deal with all this as well tomorrow. I was planning a night-cap so I could sleep.

The rain was hissing on the damaged cars.

'What's your name?' I asked, taking a pen from my lapel pocket and looking at her number plate.

'What's yours?' she sneered. 'And who put you in charge, you lanky get?'

I looked at Pippa. She might have laughed at that in better circumstances. She was talking softly on the mobile now, glancing at me.

There was a nasty burning taste in the air.

'Listen, it's simply a matter of getting all the insurance… '

'… simply a matter of ner ner ner… ' The woman was doing the sneery mimic that Pippa did when we used to argue. Only when Pippa did it, it didn't mean anything, they weren't serious arguments.

The rain was stinging my face.

'It's not just a fling.'

That's what Pippa said that night, as if somehow a *fling* would be alright. I can still see her lipstick smeared on the wine glass.

A siren cried in the distance.

The woman stood there, shouting at me, stabbing her finger. Nasty, ugly bitch. Even though we had to deal with challenging circumstances Pippa and I always kept things polite. Pippa was busy on the phone now with her back to me.

I wanted to fling that phone away.

The rain was getting harder.

The woman had her hands on her hips, spitting filthy words from her chubby lips.

Too much lipstick.

I couldn't hear what she was saying.

I couldn't hear Pippa either.

The rain was pecking at my brain. My ears were throbbing. My face was burning. I could taste acid.

Not.

Just.

A fling.

It was as if I was watching a YouTube clip.

My fist flew into her face. She fell forwards. My knee connected with her chin. Her teeth crunched. Her neck jerked. Her skull cracked with a clunk on the kerb. Blood burst from her gob as the bone bounced off the concrete. Pippa screamed.

After that it went very quiet. It's quiet now and I feel calm, but I think I might have injured my knee.

MARLBORO COUNTRY

TIM SYKES

She squeezes the surgical scissors, anxious not to injure her subject. There is precision and love in Younger Sister's eyes. She is cutting the picture out of the magazine.

'Do you have it, Elder Brother?'

'A little,' I said.

'Not enough?'

'Not quite enough yet.'

Younger Sister raises her trophy. It is an astonishing landscape: hot red rocks, white sun, orange sand, blue sky. Her face, regarding the photograph, is mad with admiration. I wheel her to the wall. She specifies the position – high in the corner, as for an icon.

I pin the object of veneration to the rugged wall, sending sprinkles of dark green plaster to the floor. I turn. Those who are awake are gazing over my head.

'Isn't it beautiful?'

'Beautiful!'

The room contains ten beds, though some are empty. Each occupant has cancer. I push Younger Sister's chair down the aisle. We stop at Grandmother's bed and stroke her hair. She closes and then opens her eyes as a restful animal does when it is touched by a trusted human. We pass between the beds. The body of First Grandfather makes a complex shape under the blanket. Uncle Vova lies on his back, arms against his sides, mouth open. He is perfectly symmetrical except for the fact that his eyeballs are both turned to the left, toward the picture.

Second Grandfather who used to be Third Grandfather beckons us. Second Grandfather is part psychopath, part silly sausage. He boasts he spent time in the camps in the thirties though he's not nearly old enough. This place isn't bound to common time. He beckons us into his confidence. His chin bristles and his eyes dart. Younger Sister glides in close enough to hear a whisper.

'Good picture,' he says. He coughs.

I help Younger Sister into her bed.

A nurse and doctor enter. They inspect each patient, speak to them, smile and stop smiling with the practised timing of an assistant and her magician. The doctor gives me some instructions and they exit.

'It is May-month,' says Younger Sister. 'White nights.'

The two windows in the room look onto a corridor, which is also painted dark green. The profiles of the doctor and nurse float past one. Then past the other.

'It's true, the white nights have started.'

'At midsummer at the home my brothers and sisters and I used to slip out and Bad Uncle Seryozha. At first it is like day but then you have grey light, which is more beautiful because it turns everything strange.'

'Don't you find this place turns everything strange?' I ask.

She doesn't understand, having never known the outside world. She is tired. Her head sinks into the pillow. I tuck her in. She shifts onto her side so she can see the picture, which continues to work its subtle transubstantiation. 'Come,' it says in English, 'to Marlboro Country'.

I tend to the others. I administer pain-killing injections to all except Uncle Vova. It is six o'clock. I swap my medical gown for my outdoor jacket and hurry out of the building.

There is a twenty-minute walk through the woods to the stop at the end of the line, where I have to wait longer than normal, then a further half-hour on the trolleybus. I get home, find no one in and eat fast. I wash and dress. I am about to leave when Dima phones. His new daughter is making an insomniac out of him but he has found the meaning of life.

Two floors down on the stairwell I meet Konstantin Sergeyich, who has again been drinking.

'Yeltsin and his Zionists won't stop until they've expropriated my war medals,' he says. 'Can you spare some notes?'

I remind him of the grave dangers of counterfeit vodka.

I ascend the Metro escalator at nine o'clock, half an hour late. Outside the station the sun is glinting on the kiosk roofs. Masha is still waiting but pouts as soon as she spots me and turns on her heels as if intending to walk away. I make some effort not to laugh. She has lovely eyes. We would be married by now if either of us had their own room.

Eventually she takes my arm. We wander the city. It is modernising: everywhere new cafés with gaudy signs, private banks, advertisements for foreign tobacco and American jeans. A vast open-air exhibition of unaffordable, needless and most desirable things.

'Look, Masha,' I say, 'soon we'll all be wearing Italian shoes and eating French cuisine every day out of packets.'

Masha objects to my sarcasm, particularly in regard to Italian shoes.

By half past ten there are fewer people on the streets, though it is still sunny. We come out onto the river. It is quite deserted: the whole Neva, the bridges, islands and the yellowy spire on the far bank are ours. We press our warm bodies against the cold granite of the embankment.

'In the future,' I stroke Masha's hair, 'we'll eat our food out of plastic packets and spend our summers in San Francisco.'

'You're quite the nihilist today,' she says. 'What's wrong with living well?'

We flag the next car. I insist on seeing Masha home, though it is out of my way. These days, I tell her, you never know whether the driver will be a professor of cardiology or a rapist. After dropping her off the driver, who overheard my quip, protests he is no cardiologist but in fact a specialist in pulmonary medicine. I tell him of my place of employment.

'An institution… I see,' he says. 'You're a doctor too?'

'No, a philologist by education. My work there is menial.'

'These days only gangsters follow their vocation. Do they pay your salary?'

'Six weeks in arrears.'

'Could be worse…'

The shadowy silence in the flat indicates that my parents and brother are already asleep. I tiptoe into the kitchen and pour water from the jug. Sipping by the window, I stand for a long while and stare at the mundane twilight.

I turn off the road, out of the woods. The institutional walls keel above me, broken windows, rust and flaking paint. Banished from sight, hopeless: majestic ruination.

Uncle Vova has died during the night. He has been removed to the mortuary. Fond, vague eulogies are said. Grandmother's gentle face smiles at me. First Grandfather again is motionless under his blanket but fabricating a quite different shape to yesterday's. It is as if he had seven elbows.

Second Grandfather is in conversation with Younger Sister.

'I witnessed his soul depart from his mortal flesh.' He flashes his row of metal teeth. 'He rose like an eagle, crossed himself and made the sign of the cross over each of us here – except for me, for I am bound for hell, for my sins…' A fit of coughs interrupts. '…then he went straight out the door. This is what I witnessed.'

He grins.

Younger Sister says she would like to imagine heaven as a place of bright golden leaf-showers like autumn at the children's home. The memory brings her happiness. Then she reclines and indicates with her eyes that she wishes for me to speak with her alone.

'Elder Brother, do you have it?'

'Yes, Younger Sister.'

'Enough?'

'Yes, enough.'

'Uncle Vova suffered very much last night.'

'I think it is better to feel intensely, even pain, than to feel nothing. Especially in one's last precious moment.'

'All the same I felt bad for Uncle Vova. I think Second Grandfather's story may not be true. Otherwise, why would his soul have blessed me?'

I too feel very bad for Uncle Vova.

'His soul understands we did a good thing,' I say.

Near evening after the nurse and the doctor have done their rounds I tend to the patients. Each receives their prescribed painkillers. However, I inject Younger Sister three times: with her own morphine, Vova's, and the dose which the old Second Grandfather gave up when Second Grandfather was still Third Grandfather.

She looks into me with a tenderness I have never seen in my world. Pure tones of feeling exist only here.

I exit the building and plunge into the woods.

Presently Younger Sister will embark on the excursion for which she has longed. She will surge into the sky and see the institution and her acquired family and the crematorium below her. She will be over the woods, shedding September leaves, and declare her kinship to the sibling geese, which are migrating. There will be seventeen colours in the sky. She will see the roof of my trolleybus. She will soar above cousin clouds and Grandfather Sun and

St Petersburg will be tiny and intricate like the workings of a wristwatch.

Then Younger Sister will descend to earth. The rock there will be red and the sand orange and the sky dazzling. Father Cowboy will say Welcome! and Where has she been all this time? and she will tell him that Marlboro country is as beautiful as she imagined.

IN REHEARSAL

SARAH EVANS

I see the two of them from the doorway, bodies cantilevered forward from the plastic chairs, their features sharpened, everything pared back to the bone. Through the glass lies the baby I examined earlier, her hair a match for her mother's, thick and dark. She doesn't seem to fit her wrinkled skin which has lost its blue tinge, for now.

I move closer, my rubber soles silent on the lino. 'Mr and Mrs Sharma?' I say. They turn as one to look at me, eyes wide and startled. 'I'm Amanda Myers, one of the consultant cardiologists here. I wondered if you'd mind coming to my office, we can talk more privately there.'

The mother's arms hug round her belly which retains its pregnant swell. Her eyes return to her baby, reluctant to sever the visual cord, and her fingertips rise to touch the glass, behind which a thin line of rust coloured blood runs up into a machine. The return line is brightly oxygenated, the appliance performing the function of heart and lungs.

I could talk to them here. Late afternoon and the ward is quiet. The babies won't listen in, and the nurse who moves between them will maintain a discreet distance. I find it easier to talk away from the babies.

'If you wouldn't mind,' I repeat.

The husband stands clumsily, his chair scrapping across the floor. He bends to support his wife up.

'Just this way.' I indicate for the couple to follow. The woman seems to have lost co-ordination and balance, leans heavily on her husband. Less than twelve hours have passed since her ordeal of giving birth.

The slow walk takes a lifetime. A strip light buzzes. Clothes rustle. Swing doors squeak. There is no small talk for these situations, nothing but my inane commentary. *Just along here; the lift shouldn't take long; not much further.*

My consulting room is cramped, my desk crowded with the computer and stacks of papers. Someone from admin has delivered new supplies, adding to the clutter. A5 pads, post-it notes and pens. Consent forms with their tang of toner. Bereavement packs, which I place to one side.

I settle myself safely behind the barriers of glowing screen and MDF, put on my glasses and peruse the medical notes and images; but I've already rehearsed what I need to say.

'So,' I begin. The mother looks down at her fisted hands, while the father looks at me directly, as if wanting to read the truth. I maintain eye contact where possible, all the while trying not to absorb too many details, so in later weeks their faces will be a blur, just one more set of parents passing through my office. 'As you know, once your baby was delivered, the hospital discovered there was a complication with her breathing.'

I picture the moment of birth, the moment which should have marked the switch from agony to joy, the baby placed on her mother's stomach, the first contact skin on skin, the first glimpse of a long-anticipated new life. The moment when – instead – the baby struggled for breath and medical staff snatched her away. And the journey the three of them would have taken, panic flashing alongside the ambulance lights, transferring them to this specialist unit.

I start to talk, gaining fluency as I do so, falling back on the technical terms that form my language, prompting myself to translate as I go along. I refer always to *the baby*. I haven't asked if she already has a name, and I don't intend to. But I remember the alertness in her eyes, her gaze so fully human, as I subjected her weakened form to the full raft of tests and scans.

'A heart defect?' The father latches onto words he knows yet fails to properly take in. 'An operation?'

I think of the fragile ribbed chest rising and falling in the incubator and how unlikely it must seem that my stubby hands might take a scalpel and carve through her new skin.

'Not exactly her heart,' I reiterate. 'But the way the arteries connect the heart to and from the lungs.' The normal circuitry is reversed, a rare anomaly. Everything perfectly formed, except for one simple yet critical thing, leaving her body starved of oxygen.

'And you can save her?' The mother speaks hoarsely, hands clasping together in supplication, willing me to be some kind of miracle worker.

'Obviously any procedure on a baby this young has risks,' I say. Never mind something as intricate as heart surgery. I tell them the percentage probabilities. Ninety percent of babies survive.

One in ten die.

It's an amazingly low mortality rate, the accumulation of determined practice; the team here has worked hard to improve the odds. It never sounds good enough.

'And if she comes through the operation?' the father asks.

I inhale, pausing to prepare myself and to alert them to the fact that the subsequent news isn't entirely good. No amount of repeat runs makes these conversations easy.

If the baby survives surgery, she'll remain in intensive care for a few days, and then in hospital for several weeks. But hopefully she could be home within a couple of months.

'She'll have a substantially normal childhood,' I say. 'Will grow and develop much in the way of other children. But her body will find it hard to deliver enough oxygen and she'll have to restrict physical activity. The procedure I've described doesn't entirely reverse her condition. It's a fix not a cure.' A somewhat messy repair, a bit of a bodged together job. 'And the bigger she gets, the harder her body will find it to cope.'

I hesitate. Wanting the impossible words to sink in, knowing they won't do, not fully, not yet. I feel like the wicked fairy at the christening.

Evening light slants across my desk forming a fractured pattern through the branches of a tree that is bursting into spring; voices approach beyond the door, vibrant with chit-chat and laughter.

'Life expectancy is around forty years,' I continue. 'Of course it's different in every case. Some live longer.' And some less long, because that's the way statistics work.

Something seems to shatter on the mother's face and she doesn't know where to look, eyes darting to her hands, her husband, the desk, the upper corner of the room, anywhere but me. She rocks herself back and forth on the chair. A night of labour followed by a day of intense anxiety and now my appalling news; it's hardly any wonder she's in shock.

'Is there nothing else....?' the father asks, his hands flailing helplessly.

My own heart flutters a little with what I'm about to say next. I've been through this several times, but I can never predict the course of words, of questions and response. I know that every nuance, verbal and non-verbal, may subtly influence the parents' subsequent decision, and I wish that wasn't the case. Perhaps the next bit would be better delivered by an automaton. 'Well...'

Their eyes snap towards me, raw and alert, frantic to hear that there might be a get-out clause, revoking all that I've just said. The bad fairy turning good, conjuring solutions out of the sterile air.

I start to talk about an alternative procedure, an untested

one. I describe it in the words that are second nature. *Aorta. Pulmonary. Systemic. Ventricle. Circuit. Transposition.* I try to simplify, but not talk down. Some parallel process in my brain assesses that the two of them are of non-European origin, but well-spoken, accents at odds with their crumpled clothes, making it difficult to judge class and education. The father keeps nodding.

I tell them how because the procedure is new, there's no proven record of success, though developments in adult surgery suggest it should be possible. It's more involved. Complex. But if it worked, it would properly correct the underlying flaw, putting the inner plumbing right, leaving the way clear for a normal life. *If she comes through.*

'And the odds in that case would be?' As usual, it is the father asking most of the questions, leaving me talking *man to man*, my natural domain of facts and figures.

'We don't have enough data for reliable statistics.'

I tread the familiar line between openness and dissimulation, choosing my words, judging how much information to volunteer.

'Any other questions?' I ask, and wait. But the two of them are still failing to make sense of anything.

'Look,' I say, and I open my surgeon's hands, asking them to trust me. 'I know this is a lot to take in and you must both be exhausted. Your baby is stable for now and I'd suggest you try and get some rest. Talk things over together in the morning. And then I'll see you again and you can ask me anything further.'

My day is finished, but I continue sitting here, looking through the scans, as if they might tell me something different. A knock on my door startles me. The door opens before I can say, *come in.*

'Not disturbing you, am I?' Tim sweeps through the doorway, bringing his aura of constantly being in an important hurry. We've been colleagues here for several years, matching each other pretty much in experience and acquired skill. In industry and doggedness. Our reward for reaching the top of our profession is that we get to deal with the trickiest of cases; we preside over more than our share of death.

'Not at all.'

He smiles in his usual hearty manner, the confident smile of a man who expects to be both revered and liked.

He comes right up to the desk, so I have to look up. 'I heard about the arterial transposition baby,' he says. 'Any decision yet?' There's something in his eyes, a glint that I might almost call eagerness. If we manage a breakthrough, it will be a first and that would be great for our careers.

'I've explained options to the parents,' I say. 'They need to think it through. I'll update everyone at the team meeting tomorrow.'

Come next morning, I'm sharp and decisive on the ward-round, impatient with the dithering of the junior surgeon who accompanies me, secure in clear-cut judgments. I dread seeing the parents much more than usual. I wish sometimes that tasks could be divided differently, so someone trained in dealing with thorny emotions could do the talking, and I could stick to diagnosis, surgery and troubleshooting aftercare. The things I'm good at. But that isn't the way it works.

The two of them reek of stale clothes, of un-showered bodies and sour milk. His chin is stubbled, her hair lank, their eyes are sunk in shadows and I suspect the night has passed in vigil, watching over their baby, desperate to believe that their love can make her strong.

Two sleepless nights. Not the best of mental states to take key decisions.

I explain everything again.

'So we don't have any choice but to operate,' the father says.

'It's only the machine that's keeping her alive. So yes.'

'And we need to choose between the two alternatives.'

I nod. I wish there was an easy answer, a clean line of advice. But there isn't. 'I know it's hard,' I say. 'Only you can decide.'

I tense against the questions that may come and I'm remembering back to a similar circumstance a number of months ago and the father asking: *how many times exactly has this new thing been tried? How many were successful?*

I looked him unwaveringly in the eye as I gave my answers.

Three.

None.

I carried on talking, saying how the figures really didn't mean anything at this stage, sometimes statistics work like that, unlucky runs. Each time we tried the operation we reviewed it thoroughly. Each time we got closer.

And each time we really do believe that we can get it right. We wouldn't attempt it otherwise.

The father didn't say anything, but his eyes narrowed. The parents opted for the tried and tested route and they asked for a different surgeon.

Three has become five.

None remains none.

I tell these parents again, how new procedures are inherently risky. How this one is incredibly involved. I do and don't want them to ask for the precise figures. I could tell them anyway.

But I don't. *The figures don't mean anything.*

The mother opens her mouth to speak. Then closes it. Milk is leaking through her grubby T-shirt. Nurses will have encouraged her to stimulate the flow, fingers pinching in lieu of an infant's suck, encouraging her to hope.

'Yes?' I prompt her.

She clears her throat. 'If it was you, your baby, what would you choose?' An appeal to womanhood. To instinct.

I keep my expression neutral. And I tell her – in absolute honesty – that I cannot answer that.

Afterwards, I drop by Tim's office. His sandalwood aftershave competes with the antiseptic floor-cleaner. He beckons me in, while continuing his conversation on the phone, 'I'll be there. Promise. Just might be running a little late.' His wife by the sounds of it, the glamorous stay-at-home wife to whom I can never find anything to say. He leans back in his swivel chair. 'I promise.' Pre-school art-works decorate his wall. A family portrait sits on his desk: two plump and contented baby twins, one each in the arms of older siblings whose faces are a-light with some silly joke Daddy will have made. I envy him his optimism.

His call ends and he turns his all-purpose charm on me, smile wide with camaraderie.

Superficially, I am merely passing on information, but underneath I know I am seeking reassurance.

'Good,' he says, then notices my face. 'Come on, Amanda,' he says. 'We can do this. You know we can.'

The operation is scheduled for tomorrow. In our team meeting, we review for the hundredth time what we aim to do and how we will go about it. We recap on the lessons learned. Both Tim and I will be attendance, alongside three nurses, the anaesthetist and the cardiovascular perfusionist. Only one of us can be in charge. Tim and I generally alternate. It was me who talked the parents through their options and in any case it's my turn.

Nigel, the newest of the nurses, stares at the coffee-stained floor and shifts from thigh to thigh.

'Do you have any questions?' I ask him. 'Any concerns?'

He shrugs and shakes his head, *no*. I start to wrap up, and then he cuts across me. 'Just how many times are we going to try this?'

I breathe in hot dust and outgassing from the synthetic carpet. Silence settles uneasily. It's my meeting; I should speak. Tim rescues me and I don't listen to what he says, but I know the substance. How every case is subjected to an after-action review and we can only decide one operation at a time.

Back home, I long to relax with a glass of wine, but I won't do so, not before a lengthy day in theatre. I sit with a mug of camomile tea, surrounded by my cool-tint walls, my orderly space. A bunch of narcissi, bought on impulse a few days ago, are starting to brown at the edges, but their scent remains sweet and hypnotic. I pick out a CD – Bach chamber works – mathematically perfect and serene. Music to revise to. It takes me back to that geeky teenager who was good with science and numbers but painfully shy. Who had no particular dextrous talents but was conscientious, hard-working and obdurate. Who always knew – somehow – that she never wanted to be a mother herself. The teenager whose youthful idealism led her to declare she wanted to be a doctor. To heal people.

I think back to years of study and of training and how through all those years, there was something that no one ever talked about, not openly, the dark secret lying at the heart of every successful surgeon.

There is always a first time.

For every trainee surgeon, for each procedure we learn, *there is always a first attempt.* And as is true of pretty much everything in life, the first time you do something, you're crap at it. No amount of book learning and cutting up corpses and watching others is ever the same as taking a scalpel in your hand and cutting through living flesh. You learn from trying, from being allowed to muddle through and sometimes you make mistakes. We practice until we get it right; we rehearse on patients.

And yes, people suffer and on occasion die as a result.

Initially, you convince yourself it's just a stage you need to get through. It isn't. It never stops. Your training behind you, you're now the one in charge. You look shell-shocked parents unflinchingly in the eye and ask would they mind a trainee assisting, and you tread that narrow line, choosing a form of words so people cannot possibly understand the full significance and you knowingly betray their trust as you shift the odds against them.

We never spell any of that out, because what choice is there? If we didn't get the chance to have a go, there would be no new surgeons.

That's life, and it isn't always comfortable.

The room is fading into darkness, submerging into shadows. The CD ends and I hear the music more in its absence than in play. My fingers tap the table lightly to the missing beat. *It never stops.*

On top of training, we dream up new procedures. *Always yet another first time.* Having a go. Pushing boundaries. Improvising our performance. Trading on a patient's faith to take unquantifiable risks.

Playing God.

If we never tried something different, we'd never progress.

My tea is cold now, the camomile turned bitter. I force it down anyway, in the hope it will help me to relax.

Just as next morning, I force down breakfast. Muesli. Orange juice. Toast. I need the fuel. I avoid caffeine and outwardly I am very calm as I drive through leafy suburbs, the cherry trees a blur of blossom. Inside, I am a mess of nerves.

I deal with a little light admin and have one final talk with the parents, before making my way to theatre. The others are already gathered in the side room. They've changed into their blue suits and caps. I meet their eyes one by one. 'Right,' I say, my voice firm, not betraying any of my fear. 'We all know what we're doing.'

Everyone nods, or says, 'yes.'

I give my go ahead to the anaesthetist and they all move through the connecting door; I'm glad for a few quiet minutes. I remove outer layers of clothing. I lather up my hands and arms with antimicrobial solution, following the prescribed system, every surface inch equally sponged. I pay attention to scrubbing my closely-clipped nails. The ritual – its precise, pedantic order – is soothing. I continue for the full five minutes before rinsing thoroughly, my hands jittering a little under the scaldingly hot flow. Water drips from my elbows.

I dry myself. I pull on the disposable cap, the face mask,

the short sleeved cotton scrub suit which covers me from elbow to ankle, the theatre shoes; I choose latex gloves in the correct size. Reflected from the glass partition in the door, I am unrecognisable, ungendered, fully in disguise.

I take a deep breath, the air thick with the aroma of rubbing alcohol, and swallow down my nausea.

I open the door into theatre. I feel like the lead-role heading out onto stage, my mind blank, but trusting that my lines will be there for me when I reach for them.

Six full-sized adults in strange clothing and masks crowd around the table on which lies an unconscious baby, her chest stained with iodine. An array of tubes run to and from her body, connecting up to drips and appliances, as if she's the living centre of some monstrous machine. An array of glittering implements are neatly lined up on one side.

Sheila confirms the vital signs. Everything is stable.

My hand wavers just slightly as Cara hands me the scalpel, though I doubt it's visible to anyone but myself. I count down. *Ten. Nine. Eight.* I seek a frame of mind in which nothing exists but this small body, its intricate physiology so bursting with life, the delicate tubing that is misconnected but which can be put right. *Seven. Six. Five.* I lay the sharp edge of the scalpel above her heart.

Fear falls away. It's the feel I would get at the start of an exam, the point when we were told to begin and my hand opened the pristine paper to see what was inside. Flight is no longer an option and adrenaline repurposes itself, channelled now into boosting my performance, not hindering it. *Four. Three. Two.*

My hand has steadied to absolute stillness.

One.

I cut. A simple slice through skin.

My hand knows the correct pressure, cutting a thin line cleanly through, enough, but not too deep. The baby has no protective layers of fat and the cut is light. Blood oozes, shocking as always in its redness.

I swab and clip. I cut and saw. The scalpels, gauze and clamps are instantly available. My fingers are chubby and clumsy alongside this diminutive anatomy and the work requires the use of finely fashioned instruments. I've rehearsed the sequence thoroughly, but Nigel gives me my cues as we go along, making sure each step is done in turn, nothing is overlooked, the very precise sequence we have worked and worked on. Everything takes time and time itself seems suspended. Things take as long as they take.

At the pre-decided points, I take small breaks, the baton gliding over to Tim, the two of us in perfect synchrony. Nigel is at the ready with a sports drink holder and I suck sugary liquid through a straw. Glucose, for energising the brain.

I feel the flow. Some less useful, self-conscious part of my mind observes how this is the part of my job I love. Like an athlete, or an actor, or a singer, everything is about the performance. About this smooth sense of being in control, of carrying out elaborate processes effortlessly, the culmination of years of practice.

Everything is going to plan. The thought seeps in, and quickly I suppress it. Like a ballet passage, or a piano piece, what is already accomplished is instant history, immediately irrelevant as it slips from present to past. The wrong step, the off-key note, the misplaced cut, the unforeseen complication, those still lie ahead as possible futures. Nothing is finished until it's over.

And abruptly, it is. Over. My hand falters just a fraction and fatigue rushes in. A glance at the clock shows we have been working for eight hours, far longer than anticipated. Eight full hours of barely moving, other than the delicate manipulations of my hands. Eight hours of full on concentration. Every muscle aches.

I hesitate only a moment, but Tim is at my side, his voice low through the face mask. 'You can go. I'll tidy up.'

I nod. I have nothing left to give. My legs can barely move

from where they've been rooted to the spot for so many timeless hours.

I retreat to the small room at the side and I reverse the ritual. Removing the gown before peeling off gloves and face mask. Very thoroughly washing my hands and arms, which are free now to tremble. Discarding my bloodied disguise and readopting my everyday look. An unremarkable, slightly dumpy, middle-aged woman.

My head aches and I so badly want to go home, to soak in a hot bath, drink that glass of wine, and hope those things will help me sleep. But there are things I need to do.

I look back through the glass panel. Tim's eyes meet mine, unfathomable above his surgical mask. He nods.

I walk slowly down the corridor, my muscles gradually reacclimatising and remembering how to move. The lift takes an age. The waiting room is at the far end on another floor.

In a replay of when I met them, I see the parents before they see me. I notice for what seems the first time how they make an attractive couple and are younger than many new parents these days. Their faces are frozen, poised between despair and hope, their hands tangled in a dual fist. For them, the flow of hours will have stuttered and stopped, snagging on interminable pause. Un-drunk cups of tea litter the table. I cough slightly. Two pairs of eyes rise to meet mine.

I cough again, something lodged in my throat. 'Sorry,' I say, an unthinking reflex. The mother's mouth pulls back in a silent scream as she clutches her husband's arm. 'For the long wait.'

I hear my voice talking about how everything has gone as well as we could have hoped, tone contradicting content so it takes a while for the parents to catch on. The elation will come rushing in at some point, my triumph of skill, this victory over death. Just now, I am emptied out and my voice emerges flat and cold, as if it was me, not the baby, who has been placed in a state of hypothermia for the duration of the operation.

'My colleague is just completing the stitches,' I explain, 'and then the nurses will settle your baby back on the intensive care ward. Once she's come round you can see her.'

I don't repeat the warnings about the next few hours and days being important. I think of the moment when the arteries – severed by my instruments – were reconnected to their proper configuration. The moment the perfusionist switched off his heart-lung machine and all of us watched the tiny miracle of the human heart pulsing bravely away, performing its proper function. I feel more confident than I ought to.

The parents turn to one another, bodies fusing together, the woman's ragged nails digging through her husband's pale shirt, both of them sobbing every bit as hard as if the news had been bad. I'm glad not to be the focus of their emotions. I hear steps outside and see Sheila coming our way. She touches my arm, administering to me with the same maternal care she uses for her young charges and their families. 'Little Maya's back in the unit,' she tells me, then nods towards the parents. 'I'll stay with them if you like.'

I'm grateful to back away.

I want to head directly home, but I don't trust myself to drive yet. I sit quietly in my office and eat the banana that will help raise my blood sugar to a better level. My mobile buzzes with a text from Tim. Time passes. I walk towards intensive care, but I don't go in. The parents have their backs to me, both angled forward to peer through the glass, blocking my own view of the tiny body with a long scar down her chest. I see only her hand, raised above her head, a small fist of determination, clinging on to life.

I carry on down and towards the staffroom and I hear the voices and laughter spilling out. Tim spots me as I hover in the doorway and he comes over, grinning and hugging me hard, the embrace badly co-ordinated so we knock uncomfortably against one another. He presses a glass of lukewarm sparkling wine into my hand. 'You were fabulous!' His voice fizzes, but there's a slight ruefulness to his smile; for all he was willing me on every second of the day, somewhere he wishes this one had been his.

'We all were,' I say. 'At least, let's hope so.' I can't seem to animate my voice. 'We've still a lot to learn.' We're still in rehearsal, with much more practice needed to get this reliably right.

I stay long enough to pass on my appreciation to each of the team, and then I make my excuses. Tim's exuberance will help counter my apparent distance.

I'm free now to leave. Stepping out into the cool air of early evening, I blink in the fading rays of sunlight and breathe deeply, liberating myself of the hospital odour of disinfectant layered over body fluids and illness. I think of Maya who has a real chance of living a long and healthy life, and of the others who – with time – will follow. I try to think only of them.

DOUBLE CONCERTO FOR TWO VIOLINS

JONATHAN TAYLOR

Based on a true story

And when she puts on the long-lost 78s, and the needle discovers the music through a forest of crackles, Rosa visibly jumps

– a jolt of recognition not just for the music itself (which she knows, used to play herself), but for one of the performers, Alma Rosé, with her unmistakable tone, technique, phrasing, *vibrato*

– all of which, despite her more-recent nerve deafness, tinnitus and, above all, musicophobia, Rosa remembers, could never forget, from long, long ago

– a terrible long-long-ago she doesn't want to remember, but which the music, and the second violinist are remembering for her...

Largo ma tanto, 12 / 8, F major, *sicilienne* rhythm, regular as barbed wire, with no up-beat, no Quarantine Block, just straight into exposition: subject theme on second violin, played by Alma, lightly accompanied by the orchestra – all heard-remembered by Rosa as it was years after the recording, in the Birch Grove, Alma standing tall, dark-haired, very thin, the inscrutable supervisor, *kapo*, number 50381, accompanied by a *Lagerkapelle* made up not just with violins, violas, 'cellos and harpsichord, but also with mandolins, accordion, flute, guitar, anything they could find in the camp, as well as the tramp-tramp-tramp of the *Kommando*s, the recorded orchestra infected with the dark future as surely as if gas and smoke might travel back in time,

the orchestra now *poco piano*, drilled by the formidable Alma back into line, F, descending through quavers E and D to dominant C, descending through quavers B-flat-A-G-E-F, heavy on the *portamento*, up to B-flat, then quavers A, C, F followed by semi-quaver run G-F-E-D all leading up to

entry of first violin – on this recording father Arnold's answer to daughter's song, and, later, in the camp, Rosa's own trembling answer to 50381's song – on dominant C above the stave, dotted crotchet tied to quaver hanging like purple-black smoke in the air, transposing the world up a fifth, into C major, descending to new dominant, G, and all the while the second violin is accompanying with counter-subject, incessant semi-quavers, rising in sequence from E to F to G to A,

like rising ('*Aufstehen*!') before the frozen sunrises of '43, from the three-tiered *cojas* into a grey room, pulling on her blue skirt, woollen stockings, striped jacket and white head scarf, swallowing metallic soup, then *Vorwärts Marsch*! in rows of five from Block 12, past the electrocuted *Stoffpuppen* hanging off the fences, three hundred or so yards to the rotting platform, outside the gates, and then the music – *Arbeitsmarsch* after *Arbeitsmarsch* for the hundreds, thousands, shuffle-marching past the orchestra to work – shivering out of her violin, diffusing, radiating, echoing,

echoing back to the barracks, where she is locked up again for twelve or fourteen hours of echoing rehearsal a day, sometimes longer, as though her *kapo* is terrified of what might happen if the musical echoes stop, the sounds and sights which might no longer be drowned out from beyond the barracks,

so the echoes don't stop, the two solo violins continue calling to each other, as if across a huge distance, across time, or through those longed-for Red Cross telegrams from loved ones far away,

until STOP

and the closeness disintegrates, the two are separated, the line goes dead, the telegrams dry up,

and the violins take turns to murmur semi-quaver farewells, ever-quieter, as if unheard by the other, in C minor,

a key which slides down into A major, pulled down,

down,

into that drowning clay mud, which seemed then to have taken over the world, sucking down still-twitching corpses, *Muselmänner*, trees, sky, memories, colour, bird-song and melody, to a place where, for Rosa at least, major keys sound dissonant, where common chords shock the ear just as much as the twitching dead on the *Leichenwagen* horrify inadvertently raised eyes

– major keys and common chords like F major, which the music has finally attained again, with the recapitulation of the main subject, apparently untouched, stoical, detached, hard-edged, always lowering gazes to the ground, never looking up into an officer's eyes, never looking beyond the nearest wall, never peering round corners or into distances, even middle distances, where five belching chimneys, rifle fire, dogs, Block 25, *Experimenteller Block*, the *Revier*, the *Leichenwagen*, the *Selektionen*, and the pesticide Zyklon-B all happen,

a musical myopia, a terminal *Blocksperre*, confining Rosa's hearing, Rosa's vision to the notes on the musical stand in front, to the strict rhythm, crotchet-quaver-crotchet-quaver, to these bar-lines, after another two of which there comes that long-held C above the stave which, again, seems untouched by what is happening around it, what has happened, but isn't really, because a recapitulation is always overshadowed by what has gone before, even or especially when it pretends not to be,

and finally, finally, the coda is ushered in *piano* by a high C on the first violin, followed by the semi-quavers of the counter-subject, somehow half-hearted, bidding *Abschied* to the second violin, which limps through the episodic material once more,

into the final triplets, *forte*, heavy *ritenuto*, the perfect cadence on a final F-major chord almost perfunctory, as though this music, with its seemingly infinite runs of semi-quavers, wouldn't find an ending if someone didn't just draw a line somewhere and say, 'That's it, I've had enough, *das Ende*'

as they did with Alma in April '44,

though for the violinist who survived, for Rosa herself, the F-major end did not come; and long after her duets with Alma had apparently stopped, long after the latter's poisoning, long after the camp had been disbanded, for months, years and decades afterwards, Rosa might still have this music's incessant semi-quavers running through her head, taking them to and from another camp, and then across a continent to a lost father's house in Great Britain, and eventually to a small provincial city in the Midlands, the notes still echoing round and round in Rosa's mind, trapped like a *Häftling* in a never-ending camp, laboriously semi-quavering for survival, not joy, with no respite, no let-up, a mental *Arbeit macht* certainly not *frei*, the semi-quavers never reaching the silence at the end of those un-applauded Sunday concerts in the Sauna, in front of the seated officers, the *Lagerführerinnen*, the *Kapos*, *Blockowas*, the shaved hordes ordered to watch and listen to Bach, hollow-eyed, hollow-eared from doorways,

and long after those hordes have been hollowed out further by memory, the Bachian semi-quavers mingle strangely, enigmatically with spectral counterpoints only Rosa can hear from the distant Sunday concerts, from the dismal work-marches, from Beethoven's Fifth, *The Blue Danube*, orchestrations of Schubert's piano music, arrangements of arias by Verdi, and – although the orchestra's music was meant to be purified, *judenrein* – even *Entartete Musik*, tip-toeing in under the noses of the officers, whilst no *Lagerführerin* was paying attention: Dvořák's *Slavonic Dances*, Mendelssohn's Violin Concerto, Mahler's *Adagietto*,

and hearing-remembering this Mendelssohn-Mahler-Dvořák-Verdi-Schubert-Strauss-Beethoven-Bach aural palimpsest now, on these old 78s, in her own head, Rosa tries not to cry with the realisation that the weaving semi-quavers aren't all barbed wire, electrical fences, cinders, ovens and searchlights

– that they aren't all glares and threats from Alma, that conductor-violinist of whom she'd been so afraid, but closed-eye nods as well, a final *ppp* '*schön*'

– that perhaps what she'd thought of as fear for the *kapo* is also a kind of love

– that the common chords, the F majors on the records aren't all dissonance or machine-gun fire, or at least not any longer

– that, after all these years of dissonant semi-quavering terror in her head, of post-traumatic *amusica*, it's not the semi-quavers she should fear, but the un-applauded silence which comes at the end of those semi-quavers:

'*Ruhe! Ruhe!*' someone is calling in her past.
'*Frieden!*'

ABOUT TIME

TANIA HERSHMAN

I'm trying to write a story about time machines. I know what
you're going to say, you with your nice face, your neat hair.
Yes, *nice*. I know that's not a word writers are supposed to
use, but I'm reclaiming it. I see you as having a very nice face,
OK? So, I know what you, with your nice face, will say. You'll
say, Don't you need to do research? Don't you need to go and,
I don't know, actually try out a time machine? Well, you know
that I am the kind of writer who does research as much as
possible, even though, yes, I do write fiction. So, I tried.

I contacted the particular authorities for permission, but
they've really tightened up. After everything that happened,
seems there's no way they're going to allow me near one. I
suspect that me telling them I was a writer didn't help, they
imagined all sorts of mischief we reprobates might get up to
were they to let us have a peek, fiddle around.

I even went and stood outside where I think they're keeping
them all, just in case. In case of what? A friendly guard, you
know. Someone to take pity on me, sneak me in around the
back, as used to happen when things were civilized, when a

person was open to bribery, when the world worked well. I stood there for a lengthy time. See? See how diligent I am? You have entirely the wrong impression of me! But... nothing.

So, after having a think, here's what I decide to do next, and I believe – although you, nice as you are, may be more cynical – that this is quite clever. I decide to contact someone who has used one. A time machine. How do I find them, I hear you ask? Weren't they all super-rich, weren't they the only ones who could afford the price? And aren't you then highly unlikely to get anywhere near one? Mostly, yes.

But then I remembered they ran some kind of contest. *Come up with a great reason why you need time travel, and you could win a trip!* I did some searching, and I found the names of the winners. Ordinary people. A whole list of them.

Clever, eh? I think you're smiling now, aren't you? Aren't you impressed by me? Well, I tracked down the one who lives nearest, I rang her up, I didn't say I was one of those *fiction* writers, I might have mumbled a bit around what I wanted to meet her for, but to be honest, she seemed keen to talk, very keen, so off I went.

She's young, by which I mean, she's about my age, which I do try and think of as still young. And she started telling me everything while I was taking my first sip of tea and reaching for a biscuit. It all came pouring out of her.

'I'm a historian,' she said to me, and she did look like she was going to maybe cry. 'The Middle Ages,' she said, and I thought, Oh no, I don't know anything about anything like that, but it didn't matter, because she was off. 'That's where... when I wanted to go. I was very specific when I entered their stupid, stupid contest. There's this plant, you see,' and here she did blow her nose and I worried a little again about the crying, but then she carried on. 'I had the exact location, they'd put the machine right there, we'd go back to one specific day, and I only needed five minutes, ten, to verify my theory that the plant was abundant in that time period. Ten minutes!'

She stops and so I say, 'What happened? Did they get it

wrong? Did you end up somewhere else?'

'No!' she says. 'They wouldn't take me. They said "Competition winners can't do *that*". They said "Competition winners get to *go a week in either direction and only in the high street.*" The high street!' Here, the poor poor woman almost wailed.

'That,' I say, 'is totally ridiculous,' and she pours me more tea and we have another biscuit, and I try and assess whether it would be OK to ask about the actual thing, the actual travelling in time. You'd be proud of me, Oh Nice One, because first, I asked her loads about the plant, whose name I've no idea of now, of course. She told me something about ancient seeds they found in some archaeological dig, but they're too ancient, they won't, you know, germinate, and all that. And there's only a limit to how much information she can get now, here.

Finally, after more tea and, for me, too many chocolate digestives, I gently ask her to tell me a bit about how it worked.

'I mean,' I said, 'you won the chance to do something only the richest got to do, wasn't that thrilling, at least?' I was trying to cheer her up.

'I s'pose so,' she said. 'And it was something. I signed all sorts of non-disclosure documents but I don't care, I'll tell you. Well, first, there was no point going a week into the past down the High Street, was there?'

'Oh no,' I said. 'That would be silly. To see last week's news and last week's petrol prices? No point at all. So you went forwards?'

'Yup,' she said. 'The machine, well, it's the size of a double shower cubicle, and no, before you ask, it's not larger on the inside. It's quite squashed. I imagine they have bigger ones, you know, luxury time machines, if you're one of the elite.' The way she said 'elite', oh boy, she was not a fan.

'How did they hide it from everyone else on the street?' I said.

'Oh, they made it look like those roadworks tent thingies,'

she said. 'All very slick.' It was then that I, your favourite intrepid writer, had a thought.

'How did they know you'd come back, once you were in the future, once you'd left the machine, the cubicle thing? Not that staying a week ahead is that much of a temptation, really.'

'You didn't think they'd let me go alone,' she said, and took a long drink of her tea. 'Couldn't possibly have eminent middle-aged Middle Ages historian on the loose in the High Street one week in the future, could they?'

I was starting to rather like her.

It turns out she was accompanied, by this weedy bloke, not some muscled bodyguard who could have bundled her back into the machine if she resisted, but who knows, she said, maybe he had hidden strengths.

'He was sweet,' she said. 'We wandered up and down, and of course it looked pretty much the same, but I could see from TV screens etc..., that it was actually the future. I suppose...' and here she stopped for a moment. '...yes, it did give me a thrill. Yes.'

She said she didn't really feel much at all during the travelling part, it was all set remotely, there was no pressing any buttons, no whooshing through space, no sensation of molecular rearrangement. Which was a shame, for me and my story anyway. We chatted a little longer and then I left. I went home and tried to write, but really I didn't have much. I still don't, and it's been a few weeks.

But then today, something strange happened, which is why I'm telling you all this. I got a message from her, the historian! I'll read it to you, because this is odd. She writes:

'Thank you so much, I can't tell you what it meant to me to receive your gift. I have no earthly idea how you did it, how you got hold of one, got the ancient seeds to actually germinate. But thank you, it's beautiful! When I opened the box, I felt a bit like I was laying eyes on my child for the first time. You have brought a piece of the past to life and I will always be grateful.'

Now, I didn't. This is the thing. I already told you I wasn't really listening to the bit about the plant, and even if I had been, it wouldn't have crossed my mind to go and try and get her one! I wouldn't know how to even start, it's not like I have extensive botanical contacts, is it? I know you're shaking your nice head with your neat hair. I know you're saying, Of course you don't, you write fiction, you spend most of your time indoors making things up.

It's all very confusing.

So, I bet you're dying to know what I did next, aren't you? Or perhaps, Dear One, you know me so well you already guessed – yes, I went to see her. Of course I did. I spent a while sitting on the wall opposite her house, wondering what I was actually going to say. And then, when I did finally knock, there was no answer. So I waited some more, assuming she would come back at some point, although of course she might have been off at a conference for Middle Ages historians, or knee-deep in mud looking for old seeds somewhere half way across the world.

Well, she wasn't, because after about an hour, during which time I had not, of course, come up with anything intelligent to say, she pulled up in her car, and when she got out and found me on her doorstep she looked both confused and pleased, which is the best combination I could hope for.

Before she even boiled the kettle I said,

'Look, it wasn't me. I didn't send it, the plant. I don't know why I didn't... didn't say something, you know, didn't...'

She didn't say anything, just switched the kettle on, gave me a strange look and left the room. I waited. She came back and handed me a card.

'That was with the plant,' she said. 'So, is it...?'

And the thing was, it was. My handwriting. Signed by me.

'No way,' I said.

'Sit down,' she said, pouring the tea. I sat.

'I don't understand this at all,' I said, and I started to feel a bit dizzy, a bit sweaty, you know, everything spinning.

'Well,' she said, 'I might have a theory. This is from you -' and here she paused and nudged the mug of tea towards me. '- but it's from you in the future.'

I'm afraid my mouth did fall open at this in a most unattractive way. But then I realised it did make a lot of sense.

'Ah,' I said. 'Yes, I suppose.'

There didn't seem much more to say at this point. We had our tea and it wasn't an uncomfortable silence, not at all. I allowed myself several biscuits, given that this could have been a stressful situation. Then she said:

'Would you like to see it?' and we went upstairs.

She had the plant in a room to itself, as if perhaps it was like a child, I guess 'nursery' is the right word for plants, too. And I have to tell you, there was something special about it. Something different, even to me, who knows, as you know, nothing at all about flora and fauna, or flora, is it? It was... majestic. As if inside its leaves it held a wisdom of years, of centuries. As if it might choose to talk, to tell us, to explain what humans are, how it all works.

She stretched out her hand towards it, but stopped before her fingers reached one of its small flowers. We stood there, looking at the plant, and then we weren't looking at the plant anymore, and we were smiling, and no-one said anything, and I realised that I was not, actually, writing a story about time machines at all.

YELLOW

ROELOF BAKKER

1

They say it's the strongest swimmers who drown.

Children from Year 4 have taken over the middle lane for swimming lessons. Their movements are robotic, manic and tight. Little arms and legs frenziedly attack the water, as if it's an evil force that must be splashed into submission.

How very different the moves are of the elderly gentleman in the fast lane. He glides through the water with vigour and elegance. I watch as he penetrates the surface gently, like an experienced lover taking his time, maintaining a steady rhythm throughout.

Hans has been coming to this pool for years. A retired actor from Berlin, love beckoned him to the big smoke. He met Peter, a costume designer from Liverpool, at a party on the set of the last Fassbinder movie.

We usually acknowledge each other when we pass on the stairs or meet in the pool: a casual nod, a silent smile, a courteous 'Hallo'.

The café overlooks the pool. The two are separated by floor-to-ceiling panes of glass, consistently grubby since the culling of cleaners earlier in the year.

I'm not consuming today. I don't eat for at least two hours before a swim. I'm just biding my time, waiting for the lesson to finish. Five minutes to go. Fingers crossed I'll have the lane all to myself.

We met here, Marek and I. I'd seen him in the pool many times: the fast lane was his domain; I belonged in the middle lane. I never imagined he'd be interested. He introduced himself in the café, asked me out.

The whistle blows. The lesson is over. One after another the children climb the chrome steps to exit the water. They hold hands and stand in twos in an orderly line by the wall.

When I look over to the fast lane, Hans isn't swimming anymore. He floats like a discarded kickboard. The children point and scream, their faces creased in horror. A stick of a girl is crying. A balloon of a boy wees himself.

The teacher acts with haste. Within a minute the children are evacuated and returned to the safety of the school changing rooms.

Meanwhile, two lifeguards have lifted the body out of the water. Hans lies on the tiled surface, lifeless like a seal washed ashore.

One of the guards performs mouth-to-mouth resuscitation, before frantically pounding Hans's chest up and down, but his efforts are to no avail.

I imagine the look of disbelief on Peter's face, when they come and knock on his door later. To break the news that will break him.

The manager shouts with authority: 'Everyone leave the café please. Please leave the café, we are closed now, we are closed.' There's a hint of a Spanish accent in her voice, or is it Portuguese?

I grab my jacket and bag, head for the exit.

Raindrops bounce off the fabric of my brolly. I'm shaken. I feel inappropriately jealous. A body offers closure. Marek's was never found.

2

Late afternoon, I look up from my book as Marek makes his way towards the sea. He leaves his flip-flops by the rock, bends over and splashes water onto his face. When the waves tease his balls, he jumps up, the shock of the cold, then dives under.

Before he heads out, he turns around and waves, both arms up in the air. His smile beams across the water like a lighthouse.

I enjoy counting lengths and swimming within the boundaries of a pool, he prefers open water: swimming without restrictions, without the need to overtake other, less competent swimmers.

The yellow cap from the swimming marathon at Dorney Lake crowns his head. He set a new personal record, came third; I finished 129th.

The hat gets smaller and smaller until it's just a yellow dot in the distance, like a Post-it note, a reminder of his existence. I go back to my book, a story based on real events, a family ripped apart in wartime.

Three chapters later – 'Assassination', 'Retaliation', and 'Starvation' – I take a swig from the flask. Green tea with a squeeze of lemon. I leave some for Marek. He must be back any minute now.

I look out over the ocean, a wide canvas of wobbling blues and shaking blacks. The sun is low, adding warm yellow and geranium orange to the colour palette. This time of the day brings such beautiful light, no wonder photographers call it the golden hour. The artwork changes rapidly in front of my eyes. What I see can't be committed to paper. Nature is more powerful than art. Art is about standing still, nature is about change.

As I cast my eyes over the glistening liquid, I don't see a bright cap set off against the blues and the blacks. All I see is water, the setting sun and the sky above.

I put my book down and stand the tallest-of-tall, on the tip of my toes. I look ahead. I look left. I look right. I observe systemically. My head moves slowly, my eyes focusing with the utmost concentration, using all my powers of surveillance. Nothing.

I scan the seascape again. My brow is tense. I'm clenching my fists and bite my lower lip. How hard can a man look?

There's no one out there.

I look behind me. My body casts a long shadow over the sand. I'm stretched out of proportion. Garish fluorescent green buckets lie on the deserted beach. I hadn't noticed the others had left.

I hurry along the edge of the water, concluding Marek must have made it back to shore. He's probably just behind the rocks, walking back over the dunes. I mustn't look distraught. I'd feel like such a fool if he saw me this way, all anxious. I fake a smile.

I climb over the rocks. When I get to the other side, I encounter no life, no man, no Marek. I shout out his name until my voice is hoarse, raspy raw. Then it gives up altogether. My shouts are nothing but little breaths of air that get swallowed up by the wind.

It's three hours since we parted. The sun has set, the sea is indigo blue, cobalt blue, navy blue. Blue turns to black; day becomes night.

I take the phone out of the bag. The battery is dead. I forgot to charge it overnight. I'm shivering. Goosebumps. I go through the motions of putting on my shorts, t-shirt and jacket, then pick up his pile of clothes, feel the cotton on my skin. Something vibrates on my cheekbone. I take the phone from his pocket. It's his dad calling. I answer.

3

A box frame is fixed to the wall above my bed. In it are the flip-flops Marek left behind. It's as if he's still with me when I go to sleep at night. The bed is like the open sea, vast and empty, daunting. I continue to have problems sleeping. I toss and turn, wrestle with the sheets, to-ing and fro-ing throughout the night. The drugs don't always work.

We were lucky to live in London. The swimming pool capital of the world has an abundance of pools. We visited nearly all, travelled across the city in the weekend, tried pools in inner and outer boroughs. The Victorian marble indoor pool at Marshall Street and the Olympic-size outdoor pool on London Fields, were our undisputed favourites. Both had been derelict for years, but had opened their doors again with a flourish.

I'm only happy when I swim. Bits of Marek live on in the water, traces of his DNA remain wherever he's done the butterfly, the breast-stroke. When I dive in, I delve into the past, back into his arms. Memories bob to the surface.

Old friends, like Jonathan who I've known since pre-school, have suggested I give up swimming and take up another sport, like kickboxing or yoga. Do something new. He says it will help me move on. Regina at work has invited me to come along to a salsa class. She goes every Thursday. I always say I can't make it. Invent an excuse.

Every day I go through the motions, fulfilling professional obligations, manically participating in the rat race. I do it all without impetus; the sole purpose is to feed myself and keep paying those bills.

I'm nothing without Marek. He was the kick in my front crawl.

4

The pretty hotel receptionist walks towards the window, with the rhythm of a samba. Looking up at the sky, she says it may well rain later. When she hears I'm off to the beach she tells me to be careful and explains Ipanema means 'dangerous, treacherous waters'.

I thank her for her advice, say 'Obrigado', and head out onto the street, 'Adeus.' I only know a few words of Portuguese.

I'd previously been to Rio with Marek, two years before his disappearance. He organised a surprise long weekend, a welcome escape at a time I was having problems at work.

He proposed to me on Ipanema beach, underneath a parasol kitted out with bunting, on the table a vase with red roses and two glasses of caipirinha. PARADISE it said on the front of his beach shorts, PARAíSO on its back. From the pocket of his shorts he retrieved a ring. I'd never even considered marriage. I said yes.

Unlike London, municipal pools in Rio are non-existent and the sea is usually too rough, too dangerous for a proper swim. No wonder all the action happens on the beach, like posing, flirting and *futvolei*, a hybrid sport mixing football and volleyball. I was happy to swim in the pool of our hotel, but Marek was disappointed. He'd envisaged a long solitary open water swim.

I arrived two days ago. I've been retracing our steps, visiting places I went to with Marek, starting at the top of Corcovado mountain, where I was again overwhelmed by the sheer size of the *Cirsto Redentor*, the colossal art deco statue of Christ, his arms spread out over the city and Guanabara bay below.

Today is my first time at the beach. I've brought the usual paraphernalia: a towel, some suncream, a cheese sandwich, fruit, a large bottle of *Serra Da Graciosa*, my passport, as well as a plastic jar containing twenty sleeping tablets.

I colonise a small piece of sand and watch a game of *futvolei*, two girls playing against two boys. The girls are winning. I mop up the energy and beauty around me. The people here are so very different from those back home, where a smile on the tube is as rare as a summer solstice.

I'm at peace with my decision. I'll go where Marek has gone before. We'll be reunited at the bottom of the ocean. I was thinking how beautiful it is that the oceans are connected, that the seas are one big family. I wonder how long before the earth will be just water, no more continents or countries.

I wash down the tablets with a caipirinha I buy from a beach vendor. I tidy up my things and cover them with a towel. Then I get up and walk down to the sea, near to where a young couple is frolicking about.

'Ola.'

'Ola.'

The water is warmer than I expected. I dive under and before I've even begun to swim, I'm slapped in the face by a nasty undercurrent. I swallow a gob of water and spit it out; I've never liked the taste of seawater.

After the initial hit, the sea seems calm, gentle like my mother, rocking me in her arms; strong like my father, carrying me, lifting me up, saying, 'Look ahead boy, there's a whole world out there for you to explore. I wonder, what you'll discover, who'll you meet.'

I feel strangely ecstatic, hysterical almost. I want to break out into laughter. I want to sing, but my mouth betrays me. The drugs have kicked in. I'm falling in and out of consciousness. I feel light, then heavy; awake, then asleep. I hear voices shouting. Waves splash against my ears, going *splish-splosh, splish-splosh*.

I force my eyes open. Blue skies. Sunshine. Crested caracaras glide past.

The sound of rotors rotating and engines roaring keeps me hanging on to the moment. Through a tiny slither of eye I spot a giant bird with a red cross. My mother speaks to me, with urgency, 'Wake up son, get up or you'll be late for school. Your brothers have already gone.'

A rescue-net drops down from the sky. I grab hold of it with my limp hands. My body collapses into the net. Before I know it I'm in the air.

I attempt to put a finger down my throat. I want them to notice I've taken an overdose. I see Marek's handsome face, looking straight at me. He says, 'Don't be afraid. Go on, go ahead. Live. Show me what you're capable of.'

The helicopter heads towards the beach. An ambulance is waiting. Raindrops tickle my bare skin. I look up. I see a rainbow, an arc-shaped artist's colour palette: red, orange, yellow, green, blue, indigo, violet.

Nature is full of surprises. It's forever changing. It doesn't stand still. Neither must I.

THE UNTHOLOGISTS

Juno Baker is a freelance writer and editor, and the lead author and editor of Cambridge University's Leading Change website. Her non-fiction has also been published by the *Guardian* and *Third Sector Magazine*, among others. Her short satires have appeared on Channel 4 and at the Ars Electronica Festival in Linz, Austria. She has performed poetry on New York's Channel 9 and supported John Cooper Clark. Her fiction has been published in many magazines and anthologies including the *Frogmore Papers, Smoke: A London Peculiar,* and the *Momaya Press Review.* Stories have also been placed in the Rubery Short Story Prize 2014, the Short Fiction Prize 2015 and Winchester Writers' Festival Short Story Competition 2015.

Roelof Bakker lives in London. He's the founder of Negative Press London and editor of *Still* (Negative Press London, 2012). His stories have appeared in *Unthology, 5, 6* and 7 (Unthank Books, 2014/15). Artist multiple *How Many Hopes Lie Buried Here Mother,* was published July 2016.

Judy Birkbeck has an MA in Creative Writing from Exeter and has stories published in Litro online, The Red Line, The Lampeter Review and Liars' League. A debut novel will be published by Holland House Books in May 2017. She lives in Yorkshire.

SJ Butler's short fiction has appeared in *The Warwick Review*, Salt's *Best British Short Stories*, *Litro*, *Paraxis* and *Untitled*. She has written and performed in a community play, overcome her fear of poetry for the Foundling Museum, and read and written for live audiences in tents, pubs and light vessels. She lives in East Sussex.

Gordon Collins has been a market risk analyst, a maths lecturer, an English teacher in Japan and a computer graphics researcher specialising in virtual humans. He has degrees in mathematics as well as an MA in Creative Writing from the University of East Anglia. He has been longlisted for the *Fish* short story prize and longlisted for the first *Galley Beggar Press* short story prize. He has had short stories published in *Riptide Vol 3*, *UEA Creative Writing Anthology 2010*, *Infinity's Kitchen*, *Liars' League*, *Unthology 3* and 6. He is currently finishing a novel 'Japan BigSYS'.

Dan Coxon is the Editor of Being Dad: Short Stories About Fatherhood (winner of Best Anthology at the Saboteur Awards 2016), and a Contributing Editor at The Lonely Crowd. His writing has appeared in Salon, Popshot, Gutter, Neon, The Portland Review, and many other places. His New Zealand travel memoir was also used as background research for a major ITV documentary. He runs a proofreading and editing service at www.momuseditorial.co.uk, working with both publishers and private clients. You can find more of his writing at www.dancoxon.com, or on Twitter at @DanCoxonAuthor.

Sarah Dobbs is a lecturer in Creative Writing at the University of Sunderland and her first novel, *Killing Daniel,* was published by Unthank in 2012. She received her PhD from Lancaster University and has taught in a variety of settings, including on the Guardian masterclass series. Previous work has been broadcast by the BBC and performed at Bolton Octagon. She is at work on a script and a new novel. @sarahjanedobbs

Sarah Evans has had over a hundred stories published in anthologies, magazines and online. Recently, prizes have been awarded by: Norwich Writers' Circle, ITT, Storgy and Words and Women: Three (by Unthank Books). Several of her stories have appeared in previous Unthologies. Other publishing outlets include: the Bridport Prize, Riptide, Lighthouse and Best New Writing. She has also had work performed in London, Hong Kong and New York.

Rosie Gailor works and lives in London, since graduating with a master's in Creative Writing from the University of Edinburgh. Her work has appeared in Pankhearst's Singles Club, Williwaw Anthology, Noble/Gas Qrtrly, Riding Light, and Anomaly Lit. As well as having had a handful of her short plays produced, she recently finished a stint as the Young Writer for The Dahl Project with Tobacco Factory Theatre in Bristol. (But her biggest claim to fame is that if you Google her, she's the only Rosie Gailor to currently exist.)

Tania Hershman is the author of a poetry pamphlet, Nothing Here is Wild, Everything is Open (Southword Editions, 2016), the short story collections My Mother Was An Upright Piano: Fictions (Tangent Books, 2012) and The White Road and Other Stories (Salt, 2008), and co-author of Writing Short Stories: A Writers' & Artists' Companion (Bloomsbury, 2014). In 2017 her third short story collection, Some Of Us Glow More Than Others, will be published by Unthank Books and her debut poetry collection, Terms & Conditions, by Nine

Arches Press. She is curator of short story hub ShortStops.
www.taniahershman.com

Tim Love's publications are a poetry pamphlet *Moving Parts*
(HappenStance, 2010) and a story collection *By all means*
(Nine Arches Press, 2012). He lives in Cambridge, UK. His
poetry and prose have appeared in *Stand, Rialto, Oxford
Poetry, Journal of Microliterature, Short Fiction*, etc. He blogs
at litrefs.blogspot.com

Mark Mayes Mark's début novel, "The Gift Maker", is
to be published by Urbane Publications in late February 2017
(urbanepublications.com/book_author/mark-mayes). He has
published stories and poems in numerous magazines and
anthologies, including the celebrated Unthology series (#5,
#9, and accepted for #10) from Unthank Books. His work
has been broadcast on BBC Radio 4 and the BBC World
Service, and he has been shortlisted for various literary prizes,
including The Bridport Prize. Mark also writes songs, some of
which may be found here: soundcloud.com/pumpstreetsongs

Jane Roberts' fiction can be found in anthologies and journals
including: Litro, Bare Fiction Magazine, Fireworks Quarterly,
Hark Magazine, The Lonely Crowd, Wales Arts Review,
NFFD Anthologies, Unthology 9 (Unthank Books, 2017).
Shortlisted for Bridport Prize Flash Fiction (2013/2016), Fish
Short Story Prize (2015/2016) and Flash Prize (2016); winner
of Bloomsbury Writers' and Artists' Flash Fiction (2013). She
is one third of the Literary Salmon team (Saboteur Awards
Longlisted, "Best Anthology" 2016).
Twitter: @JaneEHRoberts
Webpage: janeehroberts.wordpress.com

John D Rutter is a final year PhD student and Associate Tutor of Creative Writing at Edge Hill University having completed an MA at Lancaster University. He has been Guest Editor of Lancashire Writing Hub one of the organisers of The Word literature festival for three years. His short stories have been published in various anthologies and web sites including *Unthologies 5,* and *7, An Earthless Melting Pot* by Quinn Publications, *7 Stories by Edge Hill University*, *Synaesthesia Magazine, Five Stop Story, 330 Words, The Short Story* and the *Lancashire Evening Post.* He has also had chapbooks printed by Nightjar Press and In Short Publishing.

Nick Sweeney's stories have appeared in *Ambit, Eunoia Review, In-flight,* and other magazines. *Laikonik Express,* his novel about friendship, Poland, vodka, and getting the train for the hell of it, was published by Unthank Books in 2011. Much of his work reflects his continuing obsession with anywhere east of Berlin. He is a freelance writer, and guitarist with Balkan troubadours the Trans-Siberian March Band, and also plays in Clash covers band Clashback. *Traffic* was runner-up in the 2015 V S Pritchett Memorial Prize competition. More than any sane person could want to know about him can be found on his website *The Last Thing the Author Said.*

Tim Sykes is a Norwich-based writer with a background in Russian literature. He lived in St Petersburg in the 1990s, a decade of ideological flux and social dislocation for the country. His current project draws on his unreliable memories of that time / place, viewed through the prism of subsequent research of Russian modernism. Tim began writing fiction in 2013 and has stories published in Lighthouse Literature, Lakeview, Unthology 6 and the anthologies 'Being Dad' and 'The End'.

Jonathan Taylor's books include the novels *Melissa* (Salt, 2015) and *Entertaining Strangers* (Salt, 2012), the memoir *Take Me Home* (Granta, 2007), and the short story collection *Kontakte and Other Stories* (Roman Books, 2013). He is Lecturer in Creative Writing at the University of Leicester. His website is www.jonathanptaylor.co.uk.